Charlemagne Mack

Rise of the Queen

Personal Journal #1

Stephen M. Jones

PublishingWorks 2007

Published by:

PublishingWorks, Inc.
60 Winter Street
Exeter, NH 03833
603/778-9883
www.publishingworks.com

Design by What! Designs
Cover art copyright © 2007 by Sarah Chamberlin Scott

Sales:
Revolution Booksellers, LLC
60 Winter Street
Exeter, NH 03833
603/772-7200   800-738-6603
www.revolutionbooksellers.com

LCCN:2006935449
ISBN: 1-933002-41-7
ISBN-13: 978-1-933002-41-5

Printed in Canada

Welcome to my life if I had one

Ain't about a big thing, girlfriend…

…but you just might want to keep the lights on when you go to bed tonight.

All the lights.

I wish somebody had warned me like I'm warning you. If they had, then maybe when the fire roared through our apartment I wouldn't have freaked out so much. Maybe I'd have been a little smarter. Run a little faster.

And I for dang sure would've worn something other than pajamas to bed.

But let me back up a little…

A couple days before the fire, Miss McCullough—my Honors English teacher—gave my class the assignment to keep a personal journal. She said we should write in it like we were writing to our best friend. A friend who could be trusted to keep our most super-secret of secrets. And a friend who didn't judge us or keep score or laugh at things that weren't meant to be jokes.

That's how I know everything I'm telling you is the honest truth. It's the honest-to-goodness truth because when I wake up these days, they're right there—my journals. Everything's on the page, in my own handwriting, in black-and-white.

And you are the friend I'm writing to. The friend back in what I used to call "the real world."

Yo, girlfriend.

I'm about to radically, fanatically, and way dramatically change your idea of what "real" is.

See, this is how the beginning of the end of my old life began:

Imagine stuffing a size 18 gorilla into a pair of size 2 jeans and a tank top that smelled like last year's sweat. Add some really greasy-looking hair extensions and an ugly street thug attitude, and you've got a good idea of what LaZonia Johnson was like.

LaZonia was twelve years old-like me—but she had a lot of the baddest bad boys at school stone-cold scared of her.

Then there was Alana Lopez.

Alana was a lot like me except instead of being African-American with a short dreadlock hair style, Alana was Mexican-American with long black hair tied back in a ponytail with a red rubber band and she wore these really thick glasses.

We both were Honors students and had a lot of the same classes. The classes for the smart kids—the "colored eggs." That's what some of the other students, and even some of the teachers called us. We were mostly black and Mexican kids. The "colored" part came from what they used to call black people way back in the day. The "egg" part came from what they used to call really smart people like Albert Einstein and Oprah Winfrey: eggheads.

Like me, Alana was quiet and pretty much kept to herself. It was the safest thing to do at our school since most of the other kids were just passing time until they were old enough to go to jail. And it was the safest thing to do all day, every day, in our neighborhood since even the police get scared when they drive around the concrete-gray apartment buildings and shabby stores with black iron gates locked across the doors and windows. A little over a week ago in the school cafeteria, LaZonia pushed Alana's face into her Jell-O for no good reason.

While LaZonia and her bully crew of girlfriends laughed it up, Alana tried not to cry. She tried not to look at anybody. She tried to be totally invisible as she wiped off her glasses, picked up her books, and hugged them to her chest like they were the only protection she had, and walked out of the cafeteria.

I guess LaZonia saw me staring at her, so she said, "What'chu lookin' at, Punkerella?"

I pointed at her bowl of chili and said, "That."

LaZonia bent down to look at her bowl.

A fat, slimy, green toad floated up in her chili. It shot out its long, red tongue and poked LaZonia's eye with it.

LaZonia and her friends screamed. They pushed each other out of the way as they ran out of the cafeteria.

I was usually around when weird things like that happened. And because I was usually around when weird things happened, most of the mean kids didn't mess with me.

That was the good part.

The bad part was none of the good kids wanted to be anywhere near me either.

There weren't any Honors student gym classes, so everybody—nose-picking booger-eaters, finger-sniffing butt-scratchers, and colored eggs—were all mixed in together.

Miss Jablonski, our gym teacher, had gone to the equipment room to find a volleyball net. As soon as she was gone, LaZonia and her five nasty friends formed a tight circle around me.

"You the one put that frog in my chili?" LaZonia sneered.

Everybody else in the class went dead quiet. They knew LaZonia would put a beat-down on you just because she heard you breathing.

"It wasn't a frog," I said. "It was a toad."

Like everybody else, LaZonia used to leave me alone. But I guess she got tired of me being the only kid at school who was considered off limits because of my weird reputation. If she was gonna be the Top Dog at school, she figured she had to bark at me.

LaZonia brought her face real close to mine. I could smell every shower and bath she hadn't taken that week. And her breath was about a million miles away from minty-fresh.

"You think I'm playin', Punkerella?" she said. "You think I'm bein' funny?"

"Girl, I don't think you could be funny if you tried," I said. "And by the way: Ugly, dumb and in need of deodorant ain't no way to be goin' through life, girl."

LaZonia drew back her fist and shot it toward my nose. I jumped into the air, over LaZonia and her circle of girlfriends, did a tuck, and landed about ten feet away.

"By the way," I said. "How come yo momma named you after somebody's leftover Italian food?"

"At least I *got* me a momma, snake-hair!" she yelled.

When she said that it felt like somebody had kicked me in my stomach.

"Take that back," I said, feeling myself shaking.

"And what if I don't?" LaZonia said, walking toward me. "What'chu gonna do about it?"

We were almost nose-to-nose.

"Take it back," I said.

"Take this," she said, trying to punch me again.

I caught her fist in the palm of my hand and pushed her back. Instead of just falling, she tumbled through the air and crashed in a heap on the gym floor.

I landed in Principal Hanover's office.

"Do you know why I'm giving you just a one-day school suspension instead of the mandatory one-week suspension, Miss Mack?" Principal Hanover asked, trying to sound generous. It was all I could do just to keep from crying. "Your outstanding academic record is what saved you this time. But I promise you, young lady. If there's a *next* time, you will receive the full one-week suspension *and* a notation in your school records. Am I understood?"

C+⫘

When Uncle Joshua and Aunt Monique found out about my suspension they were bug-eyed crazy mad. They weren't mad at me, but at LaZonia Johnson. At the school. At Principal Hanover.

But there was nothing they could do about it.

At our apartment I wanted to throw a blanket over my head and cry myself to sleep, but I didn't have time. I had to go to my gymnastics class. And good day or bad, in seven years I'd never missed one gymnastics class. Uncle Joshua made sure of that.

The regular class was canceled for the night.

That night, it was just me and Anna Karkoff.

Whoever performed the best gymnastics floor routine would become the City League Gymnastics Club team leader for the club's ten-to-thirteen age group in the regional competitions. And the team leader always got to wear the club's royal blue and yellow club scarf at competitions.

I wanted that scarf more than anything.

I was already four points ahead of the girls in my age group—two ahead of Anna—and three points ahead of the best girl in the next oldest group.

Thirty minutes and one bus transfer later, Uncle Joshua and I were on the city's Upper East Side. This was where all the rich people lived. Where all the fancy stores without black iron gates and parks without empty liquor bottles were. Even the policemen looked happier on the Upper East Side as they cruised down the well-lit streets. They whistled as they walked down the sidewalks, nodding pleasantly to passersby. (In my neighborhood, if the police nod at you, you'd better run.)

The Upper East Side was where City League Gymnastics Club was. The building looked like maybe it had once been a library, with tall white pillars and arched windows. At night, the tall pillars were lit up and almost blinding white. There was a small fountain outside the club, and in the middle of the fountain was a bronze statue of a girl on tiptoe reaching to the sky. Sometimes I imagined that bronze girl was me and the sound of the water splashing in the fountain pool was the sound of Olympic judges applauding my gold-winning gymnastics performance.

Here, it didn't matter that Anna's family was rich and lived on the Upper East Side and that she went to a private school.

Here, it was skill that counted.

And, girl, I got me some mad-crazy skills.

I was the first to go on the floor.

I used a song called *Batonga* by Angélique Kidjo for my routine. After three minutes of tight forward flips, mid-air rotations, and sticking a really difficult reverse push-up landing, I was done. Didn't even break a sweat.

"Out*standing*, Charley," my uncle said, wrapping a towel around my shoulders as I came off the floor.

Miss Versailles, the club's manager and lead teacher, sat at a long table and quickly scribbled notes. When she was done, she looked up and nodded toward Anna, who was there with her father and her personal trainer.

Yeah, you heard me right: *personal trainer.*

Her music was by some group named Bon Jovi.

Not bad, but really nothing that got my groove going.

After three minutes, Anna was done. Her routine barely looked like it got started. All poses and no athletics.

"That club scarf's gonna look real nice on you," Uncle Joshua whispered to me.

It would have, too, if Anna hadn't been rich and lived on the Upper East Side and gone to private school.

"Surely, you understand," Miss Versailles said to us after she'd wrapped the royal blue and yellow silk scarf around Anna's stuck-up neck. "I can't risk losing one of our most influential members—"

"You mean *rich* members," Uncle Joshua said in a low growl.

"Anna's family brings a lot to this club," Miss Versailles said. "Including money and influence that Charlemagne here clearly benefits from through a full scholarship, which includes her uniforms. Is Charlemagne the best I've ever seen? Absolutely. Will she be rewarded? Most certainly. But not as team leader. Not tonight. Tonight, it is the club that must win."

You know, if there's one thing I've learned in my twelve years, it's that you should never, *ever* say something stupid like, "Oh, God! What *else* can go wrong?"

Unfortunately, between crying and gasping for air, that's all I could say on the long bus ride back to our apartment. Uncle Joshua did his best to comfort me—"Awards mean nothing, Charley. It's digging deep and giving better than your best that means everything"—but he might as well have been talking to a wall or, the way I was feeling, the piece of dirty pink gum stuck to the bus floor.

C♯

Back at our apartment I went straight to my tiny room. I got in my pajamas, flopped into bed, blew my nose a couple of times, and listened to my aunt and uncle quietly argue.

It was the same argument they'd had a bazillion times before.

Aunt Monique hated *where* we lived and *how* we lived and said we deserved better.

"It's an insult to live like this!"

Uncle Joshua believed that where we lived and how we lived was the best thing for us until some things changed. Things he never really talked about with me.

"This is the safest way for us to live, Princess—and you know this."

After a while they were quiet and I had cried myself to sleep.

Ticky-ticky-ticky… tick-tick… tickytickyticky…

Something was moving quickly outside of my window, making little digging noises in the concrete slabs of the apartment building.

I woke up, paralyzed with fear.

I was used to hearing night sounds—sirens chasing someone, thumping music from the cars, airplanes preparing to land a couple miles away, people in apartments fighting, gunshots echoing in the distance, and freighter boats with their horns moaning on the river.

But this…

…this was something…

…climbing on the *out*side of the apartment building.

The sound suddenly stopped—which *really* scared me.

Feeling my heart pounding against my chest, I held my breath and peeked outside my window.

Our eyes locked on each other.

I screamed and pushed my back against a wall.

The spider was black and furry and as big as somebody's grandmamma. With a long, furry black leg it smashed the glass of my bedroom window and crawled inside and onto my bed.

"Charlemagne Mack!" the spider hissed, its eight green eyes staring at me. "You must leave dis place at once!"

Uncle Joshua and Aunt Monique burst into my room.

Instead of grabbing me and running, Uncle Joshua looked at the giant spider and said, "Miss Lettie! What's wrong?"

"Him a-comin'," the spider said. Then it pointed a hairy leg at me and said, "A Hunter! Him a-comin' for *her*!"

"How could a Hunter find us here?" Aunt Monique asked.

"No time for questions!" the spider hissed. "Only time for running! Get gone! Go!"

Uncle Joshua scooped me up into his arms and ran. Just as we got through the door and into the dark hallway the apartment exploded into flames and smoke.

"WHAT'S HAPPENING?" I shouted.

The elevators in our building had never really worked, so with me in his arms, Uncle Joshua ran quickly down ten flights of stairs, sometimes leaping three steps at a time. Fire and smoke followed us down into the building's dark storage and furnace room, where fat bugs and hungry rats lived off of each other.

Through the fire and smoke came a voice. A cold, mechanical voice.

"You are the Orisha. You will come with me."

Through the waves of blistering fire and choking smoke that had followed us into the furnace room, I saw what looked like a man. He wore a shiny black suit and helmet.

Uncle Joshua put me down and quickly raised his hand toward the man. A bolt of white light rushed out of Uncle Joshua's hand. The blinding light slammed into the man's black suit and helmet, but he kept walking toward us.

Uncle Joshua looked at me and Aunt Monique and shouted, "Go!"

The man in the black suit shot black lightning out of his right hand. The black lightning exploded against a wall. Chunks of the wall fell on my uncle, burying him under hot, shattered bricks.

"No!" I screamed.

Aunt Monique grabbed me and turned me away from my uncle's body to face her.

She was standing in front of a bright, spinning rainbow.

"It's time to go," she said, just before another black lightning bolt exploded against a wall near us.

A chunk of the wall hit my head just as Aunt Monique pulled me inside the spinning rainbow.

And inside the rainbow…

…I died.

✳

ENTRY TWO:

Ain't from Around Here

"Am I—in heaven?" I asked. I was lying with my head in my aunt's lap and looking up into her big, dark brown eyes. I was freezing cold and my head hurt real bad.

She shook her head and said, "No, Charlemagne. We're nowhere near heaven. We're in Louisiana."

Slowly, I sat up.

My head felt heavy and I was trembling.

"Easy," Aunt Monique said. "We're in the Bayou Hatachula. About a thousand miles away from the City now."

I gently touched my head; there was a big lump just above my right ear and I could feel dried blood.

"A—thousand miles?" I said. "How'd we—"

"The slipstream gateway," she said. "All of your questions will be answered in time, Charlemagne. Right now, we must get to the Sentinel."

I could see frost steaming away from my skin and my pajamas and I felt the heavy, thick southern heat beginning to stick to me like a hot, wet blanket. Sweat started rolling down my face.

Aunt Monique stood up and said, "We have to go now, Charley Mack. There are—things—that are happening, and we need help."

"All of this—it's for real?" I said.

"Yes," she said. "Unfortunately, this is all very real."

"And—Uncle Joshua?"

Aunt Monique lowered her head. Tears fell from her eyes and splashed on the damp, spongy ground.

I put my head against her chest and cried too.

Everything felt upside down and spinning around: The giant spider at my window, the apartment exploding into flames, the man in the black suit and faceless black helmet. But the most awful thing was losing my Uncle Joshua in the blink of an eye.

He was gone forever, and I had no idea why.

I didn't even have a chance to say goodbye.

My mom and dad died when I was just a baby. Uncle Joshua and my aunt were the only family I knew. Now, with him suddenly gone I felt like I had been pushed one big scary step closer to being alone in a world I didn't understand and didn't want to understand.

After Aunt Monique and I cried ourselves stupid, we held on to each other and walked to the edge of the thick, black river water toward a rickety old wooden boat.

"*Orisha*," I said. "That—thing—kept calling me the *Orisha*."

"That thing is a Hunter," Aunt Monique said, helping me into the old wooden boat. "Terrible creatures sent out to find our kind. They either return us alive to their masters—the Purifiers—or, if we resist, they destroy us."

"'Our kind'?" I said, trying not to fall out of the rickety boat before it actually sank. "'Us?'"

"You'll know soon enough, Charlemagne," she said.

"*Orisha*," I said, lying down at the back of the boat. "That's not even my name."

Aunt Monique stepped into the boat and looked down at me.

"*Orisha* is a very old word," she said, looking way serious. "It means 'queen of goddesses.' The Hunter was asking if you were the goddess Queen of all Sky Conjurers."

After a minute I unstuck my dry lips and heard myself say, "And—like—am I?"

"Yes," Aunt Monique said. "You, Charlemagne Althea Mack, are the new Queen of the Sky Conjuring People."

I think we quietly stared at each other for a couple minutes. Then I busted out laughing. And just as suddenly, my laughs turned into gasping cries. I felt like I was going stone-cold crazy while mosquitoes chewed on me like I was the cafeteria A-lunch selection.

"This isn't real," I cried covering my face with my hands. "It can't be real."

After a minute I thought maybe if I stared out at the river long enough my head would clear. Maybe I'd fall asleep and wake up in my own bed with Aunt Monique rubbing my back and saying, "There, there—it was only a dream," and my Uncle Joshua gently stroking the top of my head saying, "We're here, Charley. Everything's okay."

Just my luck—the river was staring back at me. What I thought were large green logs floating in the water suddenly sprouted big, yellow eyes and rows of sharp, crooked, meat-eating teeth.

Alligators.

"Oh, this is *off-the-hook*!" I howled, laughing and crying all at the same time. "Be for real, Aunt Monique. Tell me I'm at home right now in bed with a fever or something. Tell me I'm trippin' on too much sugar. None of this is real, right? It can't be!"

Aunt Monique bent down and smiled at me.

Then she pinched my arm real hard.

"Ow!"

"Did that feel like a dream, Charlemagne?" she asked.

I stared at her for a long time, not liking where any of this weird, freaky, messed-up mess was going.

I finally mumbled, "Can't no black girl ever be queen of nothin'—"

"Charlemagne Althea Mack!" my aunt suddenly shouted. I felt my heart stop. "This is why I absolutely *forbid* you to listen to any more of that human hippity-hopping rap music! To begin with, young lady, 'Can't no' is a double negative. Your Uncle Joshua and I have spent *far* too much time and effort trying to teach you proper human English! I will not have *MC Potty Mouf* or *Dirty Doggy Dog* wasting *my* valuable time! And second, you were *born* to be a queen! It is your history, it is your birthright, and it is your destiny! So do not *dare* to sit there and tell me little black girls can't be queens because you, dear girl, were *born* a queen!"

She stopped shouting and her voice became a fading echo. The only other sound was the slowly flapping wings of the prehistoric-looking birds her angry voice had startled into flight.

Even the alligators gathering at the far edges of the boat suddenly wrote us off as a hard lunch to swallow. They swam away as fast as their long, knobby green tails could wiggle.

Aunt Monique knelt down in front of me, gently held my face in the warm palms of her hands, and kissed my sweating forehead.

"I'm sorry," she whispered. "I didn't mean to scare you."

"I—don't—know—what's—going on," I said between sobbing gulps of air. "And—I am—so scared."

"I know," she said.

Aunt Monique stood and walked carefully to the front of the boat. I looked around for an engine or some kind or paddle or even one of those long Tom Sawyer-type raft sticks that reach down through the water and push off the muddy bottom. Maybe the currents were just going to carry us along. But the sickly molasses-brown water didn't look like it had moved an inch in the past century or two.

My aunt spread her arms to her sides, then bowed her head and in a quiet voice she said, "*Oshun ajo*, if it pleases you. The home of the Sentinel."

The boat began cutting a lazy path through the water as if someone were rowing.

All around us were skinny trees with twisted limbs looking like the bony black fingers of witches scratching at the blue sky. Some of the trees looked as if they had been trying to walk across the river on twisted, misshapen legs only to have their feet take root in the muddy bottom.

"Okay," I said, looking around at the black water and swatting at a buzzing cloud of mosquitoes, "so if we're these powerful magicians, how come we had to live all that time in some funky old ghetto?"

"We are *conjurers*," Aunt Monique said, once again correcting me. "Magicians live in Las Vegas. Our kind comes from worlds circling faraway stars. We fell through this Earth's night sky and landed here centuries ago."

Aunt Monique had always talked real proper.

Most people back in the old neighborhood didn't think my aunt was "keepin' it real" since she talked real proper. They thought she was putting on a *front*; not being a *real* black woman. But Uncle Joshua and I knew this was just the way she was. And that was cool, I guess.

But in the rickety old boat on a bayou river Aunt Monique was talking like I'd never heard her talk before. It was way more than proper. It was just a little bit crazy and more than just a little bit scary.

I mean, sure, it's okay if *you* go crazy 'cause if *you* go crazy you won't know you're crazy because—well—you're crazy.

But it's scary watching someone you love—someone who's always been there for you—breaking the speed limit as they head to Wackytown.

"Many Sky Conjurers took refuge in some of the divided lands of this Earth. Nairobi and Nigeria, Ghana and Greece, the Australian Outback and the Great Thar Desert," she said. "For centuries we have blended in and moved with the Huldukona elfwomen of Iceland, the Shidh wizards of Ireland, and we've given voice to Mara and Laima in the Latvian forests and rivers. We have walked the cold mountains and warm valleys with the *streganonas*—the mother witches—of Italy, and we are the mists that sing on the fjords of Sweden—"

"Uh—like—wait a minute," I said. "Hold up. That part about *us* coming from 'worlds circling faraway stars'? That's just what my English teacher Miss Jacoby calls a metaphor, right? 'Cause, I mean, you told me we moved to the City from Cleveland. So okay, I mean, if we *did* come from a different planet, then that would make me—us—"

Aunt Monique turned slightly and looked at me.

She was smiling.

I didn't have a good feeling about that smile.

"Let's just say we are definitely not from around here," she said.

ENTRY THREE:

The Sentinel

It felt like hours before Aunt Monique and I spoke again. It may have only been a few minutes, but the hot, humid air slowed everything down, including time.

I was still pretty sure this was all a dream, so I thought I'd break the silence and quiz my aunt a little more. I mean there *had* to be a flaw in this Alice-In-Wuzupland nightmare that would trigger waking me up, right? And the way to find the flaw was to ask questions. Then, poof! Dream over, nightmare gone, back to stupid old gym class and smelly LaZonia Johnson, right?

I said, "Okay, so if we're these witches and warlocks from other planets, couldn't we have whipped up a spell or two that put us in a for-real house with for-real trees and a for-real lawn with maybe a for-real dog or something?"

"Our poverty was by choice," she said, without looking back at me. "Joshua's choice. Wealth and possessions are all the things Hunters look for when they search for our people on worlds we've escaped. Worlds where our powers might seem impossible or dangerous or somehow evil. Sky Conjurers who use their powers to create wealth call attention to themselves. They endanger themselves and they endanger us all. Joshua was certain that our hiding among the poor was most effective because on this Earth, the unfortunate poor far outnumber the monied fortunate."

"Yeah, well I still say I'd rather face one of those Hunter dudes straight-up than live the way we did every day," I said. Guess I was feeling a little grumpy from the heat. For a dream, this heat was getting on my last nerve, girlfriend. "I mean, I got kicked out of a *bad* school in a *crummy* neighborhood when all the time—some abracadabra! A little shazam!—and I could have been kicked out of a *good* school in a *good* neighborhood!"

"Were you ever hungry?" Aunt Monique asked, without looking back at me.

"Well, no, but—"

"Did you ever feel unloved?"

"No, but see—"

"Were your clothes ever threadbare or dirty?" she said. "Were your shoes ever full of holes? Was your winter coat not warm enough?"

"You know what I'm saying," I said getting, like, really annoyed. "No, I'm afraid I don't know what you're saying," Aunt Monique said, turning to me. "It seems the only poverty you've suffered is not having enough gratitude for the life you have been truly blessed with."

Aunt Monique turned her attention back to the black water ahead of us.

"Yeah, well a new pair of Adidas every once in a while would've been nice," I grumbled to her back.

We were quiet the rest of the way.

After a few minutes more, Aunt Monique pointed to the shore and said, "The home of the Sentinel."

I looked over at the shore, squinting, trying to catch a glimpse of a house through the tangle of trees and dark bushes. Finally, I saw what looked like a small, gray outhouse that was maybe one summer storm away from being blown into a bazillion toothpicks.

"Oh, you have just *got* to be kidding me," I said.

The boat slipped up on the shore and we got out.

Aunt Monique bowed to the rickety old boat and said, "Thank you for your guidance and patience."

"I am grateful for your humility," the boat said in a deep, sleepy voice before sliding back into the water and slowly drifting back down the bayou river.

I looked up at Aunt Monique, not knowing what to say or think. She smiled down at me and said, "Boat people. Very nice once you get to know them."

Then she turned and began walking through the tangled dark forest toward the small, gray outhouse half hidden by trees that looked like bark-covered skeletons frozen in a terrifying dance.

So here I was supposed to be some sort of queen and I was walking to an outdoor bathroom in the middle of a steaming hot nowhere!

On the door of the outhouse was a very detailed carved wood face, eyes closed like it was sleeping. The face was long and skinny and had a beard that wrapped around the wooden door handle. Why anybody would waste a carving like this on the door of an outdoor bathroom was beyond me, girlfriend. I mean this wasn't exactly the kind of fairy-tale castle or magician's fortress I'd ever read about.

I leaned in close to the door to take a closer look at the carving. I couldn't take my eyes off of the details of the carved face—the face of a bearded old man. There were little flowers that peeked through the long beard and strange symbols carved into the dreadlock braids pouring from the top of the figure's old-man head.

"Wow," I whispered. "That hair is just like mine!"

"I like it, too," the elderly wooden man's face said. His gray wooden eyelids opened. "Of course, out here a good moisturizer is hard to find."

I screamed, stumbled backward, and fell on my butt.

"We seek refuge, Sentinel," Aunt Monique said to the carved face on the door.

"There are many troubling things transpiring," the wooden man in the door said. "Only one of you will be admitted. The other must pay for that admittance with their life. Choose now or leave."

"Say *what*?" I said, picking myself up and brushing myself off. "You mean somebody's got to *die* just so the other person can get into this fallin' down Porta Potti? No way! Let's roll, Aunt Monique! We *gone*!"

I turned and stormed away from the door, ready to walk as far as I had to. Baton Rouge. New Orleans. Cleveland. Where-*evah*, girlfriend, where-*evah*.

I turned just in time to see my aunt kneel down in front of the door.

"The girl is our future," she said, her head bowed. "I am the past. Admit her and take my life as the ticket for her admittance."

"No!" I shouted.

"So be it," the door said.

I ran back and began banging my fists against the wooden face on the door.

"You are *not* taking my aunt away!" I shouted, punching at the wooden face on the door. "Somebody just took my uncle from me and I am not gonna be left here all by myself! You want to mess with somebody, mess with me, ya poop-faced fool!"

"Seriously?" the door said.

"What'chu mean 'seriously,' fool?" I said, taking an exhausted and confused step back. "I'm as serious as a heart attack!"

"You shall both pass," the face in the door said.

Suddenly there was the clanging and rattling of locks unlocking and bolts and chains and gears whirling and clickety-clacking. A lot of security for a bathroom in the middle of the woods.

"You mean that was a test?" I asked.

The wooden carving of the man's face nodded sadly. "You'd be amazed at the number of people who would give up the life of a friend to save their own skin," he said.

"No," I said. "I wouldn't." I gave his wooden nose one final bang with my fist and said, "Your job sucks, mister."

"It's a living," the carved face sighed.

The door of the outhouse creaked open and a sliver of a black man's face peeked through. His one wide-open eye darted from me to my aunt and back to me again.

Suddenly the door flung open wide and a tall man with a long white beard said, "Come in! Come in! Hurry! No wasted time! None! Not a second! Not a nanosecond! Wipe your feet! Come in! Come in!"

I held my nose and entered the outhouse with Aunt Monique following behind me.

Once we were inside, the door slammed shut and began locking, bolting, and chaining itself. Aunt Monique bowed to the tall man with the long white beard and said, "Charlemagne, this is Mr. Efrim Ecclesiastes Trinidad. The Sentinel."

Mr. Trinidad—the Sentinel—bowed low to me and said, "I am honored, your Highness, though it had been my wishes, hopes, and prayers that you would not ascend to the throne in such a truly awful and life-threatening manner." Having just walked into an outdoor bathroom, I was beginning to wonder what kind of throne the brotha was talking about.

Mr. Trinidad took my aunt's hand in his, bowed again, gave her hand a quick kiss and said, "Princess, of all the powers I have been granted, it is the power to restore life that I lack. I am most sorry for the loss of your sister, Queen Yolanda. And now this bitter and tragic news of Ashanti Kai Joshua. I would gladly have traded my life for theirs."

Aunt Monique nodded and I saw tears flooding her eyes again.

"Come, come, come," Mr. Trinidad suddenly said. "We've no time to lose. None. Not a flickering ember of a second. This outpost has been compromised."

Mr. Trinidad turned and walked quickly away from us through a blue darkness that smelled like cool vanilla and lilac. It was the cool vanilla aroma in the air that made me realize two things:

1. We weren't in the awful bayou heat anymore, and
2. The outhouse was bigger inside—*impossibly* bigger!—than it looked from the outside.

"This can't be," I said looking around at the huge, dark blue room Mr. Trinidad, Aunt Monique, and I rushed through. Just ahead of us there was a long blue velvet sofa that seemed to glow. The sofa was winding every which way through the room. Occasionally along the sofa's winding path, a long glass table with glowing fruit appeared. Or a big pink vase with yellow flowers that seemed to be humming. Above us there were hundreds of candles floating where a ceiling should have been. White doves fluttered everywhere and a few even landed for a short time on Mr. Trinidad's shoulders.

"I hope you like what I've done with the place," Mr. Trinidad said, hurrying ahead of us. "After a couple hundred years, you get ideas."

A baby elephant appeared out of the darkness and crossed our path. It wandered up to Mr. Trinidad and unfolded its trunk. Mr. Trinidad pulled a white envelope from the pocket of his long purple robe and handed it to the elephant. The elephant wrapped its trunk gently around the envelope and quickly trotted away.

"Unbelievable," I heard myself say.

"The only thing unbelievable, your Highness," Mr. Trinidad said, still walking quickly ahead of us, "is the human capacity not to believe in the unbelievable for very long. Then again, this outpost is quite a lot like people, don't you think? It doesn't quite matter what people look like on the outside. Each person has a million unbelievable rooms inside, waiting to be discovered."

"S'up with the elephant?" I finally said.

"Ah! Yes! Cheddars. Cheddars lives with a fellow Sentinel in India," Mr. Trinidad said. "We trade e-mails."

I stared at him, not knowing if this was a bad joke or just a really bad postal system.

"Are you on some sort of medication?" I asked.

"Charlemagne!" Aunt Monique snapped. "Do not get beside yourself, young lady!"

Mr. Trinidad laughed and said, "No, it's quite all right, Princess. Miss Charlemagne is quite refreshing even if we might all die horrible deaths because of her."

I stopped walking.

"Horrible—deaths?" I gulped. "Uh—what exactly does that mean?"

"It simply means," the Sentinel said, still walking quickly through the echoing darkness, "that the Hunters will erase from existence anything and anyone in their way if it prevents them from getting to you."

"'Erase from existence'?" I repeated, feeling my mouth go dry. "And what's with the 'if' part? How big of an 'if' are we talking about?"

Mr. Trinidad stopped walking, turned, and closed his eyes briefly. It was then that I noticed he looked exactly like the face carved in the outhouse door, right down to the small flowers growing from his long white beard.

Mr. Trinidad thoughtfully stroked his beard. "How big of an 'if'?" he said absentmindedly. His bushy white eyebrows began quivering and he began walking in a small circle, talking to himself. "Interesting question. Let's say we use the square-root of Never over an exponential factor of Always, times Sometimes with a differential of Maybe, then the exponent of *If* becomes a component of geometrically expanding Fractals meaning—meaning—"

"Meaning what?" I was not having a good feeling about much of anything at the moment. I needed to know what my odds were of getting out of this thing alive—whatever *this thing* was.

"Meaning," Mr. Trinidad finally said, "you should never think of the odds of *If*, your Highness. The minute you start to worry about the odds of *If* is the second you give up on Doing, Did, Done."

He turned quickly on his heels and walked away from us further into the blue darkness muttering, "Come, come, come! Not a moment to lose!"

I turned and look up at Aunt Monique. "He's a couple ounces short of a two-liter bottle of Coke, isn't he?"

"If you mean odd, then yes—he is a couple ounces short of a two-liter bottle of Coke," she said. "He's been this way since I've known him."

"And, like, how long would that be?"

"Christmas," she said, "1793."

ENTRY FOUR:

Born for What

I was out of breath when we finally caught up with Mr. Trinidad. We entered a huge, round room full of soft echoes and distant whispers. I looked up. The deep purple ceiling was high and round and looked like one of those big cathedral churches in Europe or Ghana that I'd seen pictures of. Blue and orange and red lights pulsed softly against the purple ceiling. I looked at the floor. It was a very black, shiny marble floor with silver glitter. The floor was strange because even though it was shiny, I couldn't see my reflection in it. I felt like I was standing in the middle of outer space. Kind of a creepy feeling that had my stomach doing gurgling somersaults.

"Yes, yes, yes," Mr. Trinidad said looking up. "Here she is."

Slowly lowering itself on a silver thread from the high dark ceiling was the furry black grandmamma-sized spider Uncle Joshua had called "Miss Lettie."

I screamed and grabbed Aunt Monique.

"It's all right, your Highness," Mr. Trinidad said. Looking up at the giant black spider spinning down from the ceiling he said brightly, "Feelin' good, Sister-Woman Lettie?"

"Feelin' fine, Brother-Man Efrim," the spider said. Then Mr. Trinidad turned to me, grinned, and said, "I just love the way she enters a room!"

Frankly, I wasn't a big fan.

Soft waves of purple and green light washed over the spider as it spun down the silver thread, changing into a really pretty caramel-brown woman with thick, wild black hair that fell in loose curls over her shoulders. She was wearing a chiffon dress that fluttered like a rainbow-colored cloud around her as she lowered herself to the floor on the shimmering thread.

"Of course, you remember Miss Lettie, your Highness," Mr. Trinidad said.

"Yeah," I said. "Not like this though."

Miss Lettie was older than my aunt. She stood in front of me, crossed her arms over her chest with her hands on her shoulders, bowed low and said, "Your Highness." Then she bowed to Aunt Monique and said, "Princess." It was only then that I noticed Miss Lettie's thick Jamaican accent. It was the kind of accent that sounds like it's made from honey and black pepper and blue water and sunshine.

Guess I'd been too scared to notice her accent before.

"Your arm," I said. "It's bleeding."

"Not for much longer," Miss Lettie said. "It be a little token from de Hunter who come for you, your Highness."

"Let me have a look at that," Mr. Trinidad said, taking hold of Miss Lettie's arm. He examined the gash and made a serious grunting sound. "Infected with Dark Matter. Even your extraordinary healing powers are failing against the infection." He looked up from the wound at Miss Lettie and said, "The arm—it may have to come off."

"Wait a minute, whoa!" I said, feeling my knees go weak. "You mean like—*cut* it off? *Here*?"

"I'm afraid so," Mr. Trinidad said.

"No way," I said turning and walking away. "I ain't about this. Where's the door? I'm out."

"Charlemagne!" Aunt Monique called. "Whether or not Miss Lettie's arm goes or stays is of no importance. But if you go, you just might be killing us all. The Hunter found us back in the City. How long do you think it would take him to find us here?"

I could feel hot tears rolling down my cheeks. I said, "You people are supposed to be *magicians*, for cryin' out loud!"

"Conjurers!"

"What-*evah*! And now y'all talkin' about choppin' somebody's *arm* off? That is *seriously* messed up! I'm going home—"

"There is no home to go back to, Charlemagne!" Aunt Monique said.

"Your Highness," Mr. Trinidad called out to me. "It is possible *you* could save Miss Lettie's arm. Perhaps even her life."

I stopped.

I started shaking and crying and gasping for air.

"You got the wrong girl, Merlin or whatever your name is," I said. I was thinking again about having just lost my uncle. I was thinking about losing the floor exercise team leader position to that snot-nosed Anna Karkoff. And I was thinking about getting kicked out of my crummy school. And I was thinking about losing my mom and dad before I even had a chance to know them.

And now I was supposed to be some sort of great and grand witch? A conjurer? Some off-the-hook freak who could save a grown woman from losing her arm?

"Without your help, she may ascend," Mr. Trinidad whispered to me.

"You mean—die?"

Mr. Trinidad nodded slowly.

I lowered my head. "I couldn't save my uncle," I said. "What makes you freaks-of-the-week think I can help her?"

"Got lots of tings boilin' and bubblin' inside ya, eh?"

I looked up. It was Miss Lettie talking to me.

"You don't have to do no-ting you don't want to do, girl-girl," Miss Lettie said.

I glanced at her arm. The deep gash was bleeding and beginning to glow a sickly yellow. Inside the wound were small, oily black droplets swirling around, joining together and growing larger.

Dark Matter.

"Does it hurt?" I asked.

"Feels cold," Miss Lettie said. "Like fear."

"What'll happen if it—you know—"

"I will ascend."

"Die," I said.

"No," Miss Lettie said. "I mean someday I will leave dis body. All dat my spirit be and promise to be gonna rise to a life above and beyond dis body."

"Yeah, right," I said. "That's just a nice Sunday-school way of saying you're about to become a boxed lunch for worms."

We looked at each other for a long time.

Then I said, "I don't even know who I am any more."

"Den maybe time come to know who you really be," she said, smiling at me.

I walked back with her to where Aunt Monique and Mr. Trinidad stood. They were all looking at me.

"I—I guess I could try," I said to them. "But don't blame me if things go bad on this one, y'all. I've never done this before."

I wasn't even sure what "this" was.

"Neither have we," Mr. Trinidad said with a grin and a wink. "All we have is our faith, your Highness. Isn't that all one really needs?"

"That," I said. "And maybe some Neosporin."

Aunt Monique stared at Miss Lettie as if Miss Lettie were the one person on Earth she didn't want to help.

All of us gently laid hands on Miss Lettie. I heard Miss Lettiewhisper to my aunt, "I am truly sorry for the loss of your sister, Princess Monique."

"Perhaps she would still be alive if she had put her trust in a better teacher," Aunt Monique whispered back.

"Let's begin," Mr. Trinidad said.

Miss Lettie looked at me. Tears flooded her eyes and she said, "I be sorry for all de pain I've caused you, your Highness."

I had no idea what she was talking about, but it looked like she was hurting a lot, and not just from the infected and bleeding gash in her arm.

Mr. Trinidad and Aunt Monique and Miss Lettie began singing:

Sara yeye bakuro,
Sara yeye bakuro
Orisha Pachamama, sara yeye bakuro ...

I closed my eyes and felt the sound of their voices rippling over and through me like cool water. I didn't have a clue what they were saying. But, okay, so here's the really freaky part: I heard me singing the same words *they* were singing!

I had no idea what I was saying. For all I knew I could have been ordering a chili-fries and a Pepsi.

After a while the tiny little corner of my mind that was quietly freaking out noticed something: I was the only one left in the room who was still singing. It was just my voice, but even then something weird was happening to my voice. It was splitting, changing into three different voices singing three different octaves.

I opened my eyes.

Miss Lettie was floating in the air in front of me, her body wrapped in sheets of a shimmering golden glow. Light danced around her body, flowing into the wound in her arm and out again.

Then I saw where the golden light was coming from.

My hands.

Out of the corner of my eye, I saw Mr. Trinidad and Aunt Monique. They were staring at me with wide, unblinking eyes and their mouths hung open.

I couldn't speak.

I couldn't move.

All I could do was hear my voices singing and watch Miss Lettie floating inside golden light that was coming out of my hands.

My mind was telling my body to run. To scream. To squeeze my eyes shut and deny everything they were seeing. My heart was saying the opposite. It was saying, "Be cool, girl... everything's cool..."

"Like her mother," Mr. Trinidad whispered to Aunt Monique.

"She was born for this."

"She truly is the Orisha," Aunt Monique said in disbelief.

Thick, black oil—the Dark Matter—began dripping out of the gash in Miss Lettie's arm and splashing onto the floor.

The Dark Matter frantically whipped itself into half of a Hunter's black helmet. The helmet gave a high-pitched screech, then melted into a black puddle. The puddle tried to form itself into a Hunter's boot. Again, it gave a horrible screech and the boot became a black puddle. The puddle shaped itself into a gloved hand. The hand tried to pull itself along the floor. Just before it reached my foot, it became a black puddle again.

Then, it burst into flames and was gone.

I'm pretty sure I fainted after that.

ENTRY FIVE:

The Lion and the Goat

"The history of our world is a history of slavery," Miss Chisholm once said in my Honors History class. "For thousands of years, people on this Earth have enslaved the bodies, minds, and spirits of each other. Even today slavery is one of humanity's greatest and most urgent challenges. Ask yourself tonight how much of a slave you are. To TV. To pop music. To feeling like this neighborhood is all you'll ever know of life. Begin your journey to freedom tonight, class, by turning off your TV and reading a book."

Ms. Chisholm was only part right about slavery.

Slavery wasn't just human history.

It was the history of planets and people way beyond any of the stars you might see tonight...

When I woke up, I wasn't in Miss Chisholm's class. I was lying on the black marble floor. Kneeling by me were Aunt Monique, Miss Lettie, and the Sentinel.

The Dark Matter infection on Miss Lettie's arm was gone.

"Will someone please tell me what's happening to me," I pleaded in a voice that sounded small and scared, like a baby mouse cornered by a hungry cat.

Mr. Trinidad stood, bowed low to me, and said, "You are more than you ever imagined yourself to be. And you will achieve more than you ever thought possible. You truly are Queen of the Sky Conjurers." I started trembling. I was crying again. I was scared and confused and I felt lost—everything I'd promised myself I'd never be, couldn't afford to be, because cities don't have mercy, and most people don't know pity.

"It's too much for her," Aunt Monique said. "She needs more time—"

"Time, unfortunately, be one precious ting we out of," Miss Lettie said, stepping forward. "We must protect and train her now. De Hunters have already begun to—"

"It's all because of *you* that we're in this mess!" Aunt Monique shouted at Miss Lettie.

"I very much doubt Miss Lettie had anything to do with our current situation," Mr. Trinidad said.

"You know what I mean," Aunt Monique growled at Mr. Trinidad. "If this woman—" she pointed angrily at Miss Lettie, "had done her job right in the first place—if she had properly taught my sister—"

I could see Aunt Monique's eyes filling with tears.

"I understand how you feel, Princess, but—" Mr. Trinidad said.

"You understand *nothing*!" Aunt Monique shouted as tears ran down her cheeks. With her finger still pointing at Miss Lettie, Aunt Monique said, "The future died with my sister—and this one—Miss Lettie—she is to blame. You know this. We all know this!"

"Believe what you will about Miss Lettie and the past, Princess," Mr. Trinidad said. "Whatever you believe will not help us in this present and most urgent situation. Someone—a Sky Conjurer with a very high security clearance—hacked into every Sentinel outpost system on Earth and sent a signal for the Hunter who attacked you. The signal was a barely noticeable carrier beacon disguised by our own long-range sensors. I can only assume this beacon reached a remote Hunter Scout on the edge of the star frontier and alerted it as to Miss Charlemagne's location here on Earth."

"Dat be impossible," Miss Lettie said, still a little weak from her healing. "No Sky Conjurer even with de highest security clearance can access a Sentinel outpost."

"You can," Mr. Trinidad said. We all got quiet and stared at Miss Lettie. "So can you, Princess Monique—"

"This is ridiculous!" my aunt shouted.

"The only other Sky Conjurers capable of accessing a Sentinel outpost are members of the council, the Ashanti Kai Joshua, and—him," Mr. Trinidad said.

I looked around. There was no one else in the room except for Mr. Trinidad, Aunt Monique, and Miss Lettie.

"Him?" I asked. "'Him' who?"

Mr. Trinidad looked nervously at Aunt Monique and Miss Lettie before looking at me.

"Morabeau," he finally said. "Another Ashanti Kai Knight like Joshua. Together, they were assigned to protect you, your Highness, and the other Sky Conjurers exiled here on Earth."

"Maybe y'all haven't noticed, but this is one big 'ol blue rock dancin' on the beam," I said. I was talking about the planet Earth orbiting around the sun. "And y'all only had *two* brothas protecting me and everybody else?"

Mr. Trinidad shrugged and said, "Why flex all of your muscles when just a few will do?" Then he said, "For painfully sad reasons, Joshua is not here to defend himself. But as an Ashanti Kai Knight assigned to protect the royal family, Joshua certainly had certain Sentinel outpost privileges just as you do, Miss Lettie, and you also, Princess Monique."

"Why would my uncle call up somebody who would hurt him?" I said. "That doesn't make sense."

"And why Morabeau?" my aunt said. "Surely he has acquired enough money masquerading as a human to have lost any interest in the cause of the Sky Conjuring People."

"Money, dear Princess, does not mean power," Mr. Trinidad said. "And it is power that Morabeau still thirsts for."

Miss Lettie said, "Yes, Morabeau be dangerous. But I doubt him be seeking power from de same creatures who could destroy him in de blink of a dark crystal eye."

"Then it seems you should question the *teacher* first!" Aunt Monique said angrily, pointing her finger at Miss Lettie.

Miss Lettie bowed her head and said, "On my honor, Princess—whatever history 'tween you and me, I would never summon powers dat would destroy us. Our bickering does not change de fact dat dis child—" she pointed to me "—our new queen—be in very grave danger."

"Hey, listen up, y'all," I said standing on rubbery, wobbly legs. "Somebody'd best give me the 4-1-1 right now, n'k? 'Cause if you don't, then I am *seriously* out of here and y'all can do all this interplanetary smackdown thang without me."

Mr. Trinidad gave my aunt and Miss Lettie a look and said, "We will only survive this together, my sisters. I beg of you to make peace in this moment for the sake of the child."

Slowly, Aunt Monique and Miss Lettie nodded to Mr. Trinidad.

Then they bowed to each other.

"Forgive me, sister-woman," Aunt Monique said to Miss Lettie. "For the sake of our queen, I am your friend and ally."

"Forgive me, sister-woman," Miss Lettie said to Aunt Monique. "For de sake of our queen, I am your friend and ally."

"Will you please tell me what's going on?" I said to Mr. Trinidad. I was about a split-second from losing my last bit of sanity.

Mr. Trinidad nodded, smiled, and said, "Perhaps I can shed some light on our situation."

He raised his right hand and a glowing ball of orange and blue light spun to life in the palm of his hand. He tossed the ball of light into the air. It exploded and the room was suddenly filled with thousands of spinning stars, rushing meteors, and glowing orange and purple clouds where baby stars were being fed before being born into outer space.

Mr. Trinidad told me about star systems and planets way beyond where even the Hubble Space Telescope could see or poets had ever imagined. Places where people farmed and made wonderful music and were at peace with other worlds.

Then they came.

The Purifiers.

At first they only wanted knowledge of the magical ways of these people. But learning takes time and patience, and the Purifiers had a faster schedule in mind. Libraries were the first things the Purifiers snatched up. And when the libraries refused to give up their secrets of sorcery and magic, the Purifiers took the people who might unlock those secrets. As their search for the knowledge of magical ways grew, so did their hunger and greed for more. They enslaved whole planets, turning families into slaves. They ripped apart the land and drained the seas of a thousand worlds in search of magical stones and metals and waters and plants.

Now they wanted me.

They were the ones who had sent their army of Hunters in Dark Matter suits of armor into the endless cold of space searching for me.

But it wasn't even me they wanted.

They wanted something called the Star Charm. A necklace that only the Queen of the Sky Conjurers could wear. A necklace that long-ago stories, fading legends, and nearly forgotten myths said was filled with the conjuring power of a thousand magical worlds and a thousand powerfully enchanted goddesses.

Goddesses from some of the faraway worlds escaped the Purifiers and landed on Earth centuries ago. They were goddesses I'd heard about. Read about in library books. Goddesses from Egypt and Nigeria, India and Greece, Brazil and Mexico, Ghana and America. Goddesses who were now just silly little bedtime stories for silly little girls like me ...

Yemaya and Maat, Shakti and Kali, Isis and Cerridwen.

My mother had been their protector.

She had been their queen. Their leader.

And now she was gone.

Before the Hunters found my mother, she had hidden the Star Charm.

Aunt Monique blamed Miss Lettie for not training my mother properly in something called "enchantment defense." And she blamed Miss Lettie for not teaching my mother how to fully call on the goddess powers of the Star Charm. Powers that maybe could have saved her life.

"Miss Lettie was the greatest of all Royal Court Governesses," Mr. Trinidad said, pointing to a star that he said my real home orbited.

"Governess," I said. "That's like a teacher, right?"

"Yes," he said. "Unfortunately, she got herself into some—how shall I put this delicately?—difficulties."

We walked through the field of stars away from Aunt Monique and Miss Lettie, who were at far opposite ends of the room. They had apologized to each other with words, but there was still something very uncool between them.

"A governess of the Royal Court takes a vow—a very special and very serious vow. When they accept the extraordinary role of Royal Court Governess, theirs is only to teach. To instruct. They must never become directly involved in the lives of their students beyond lessons."

"That's not a teacher," I said. "That's a computer."

"Precisely what Miss Lettie thought," Mr. Trinidad said, "though she didn't quite put it as eloquently as you, your Highness. Especially when it came to your mother. Your mother was very special. Perhaps the greatest of all Sky Conjuring queens in the past thousand years. With her greatness came great danger. She helped millions—perhaps even billions!—of conjuring people from other planets escape the Purifiers. She hid them on worlds far from the Purifiers and their army of Hunters. She risked her life as no other queen had for the safety of others." We stopped walking for a moment. I watched the tiny stars and little planets and miniature meteors rush between Mr. Trinidad and me. "Miss Lettie saw this extraordinary quality in your mother very early on. She also saw the great personal danger this special quality invited. Instead of leaving the safety of the queen to her assigned protectors—her Ashanti Kai Knights—Miss Lettie became directly involved. She secretly formed an alliance with the man you know—knew—as Joshua. Trained him in very special conjuring arts to be the best of the best Ashanti Kai Knights, all in an effort to protect your mother. And this is something a governess—a teacher—must never do."

"Even if it means saving people's lives?"

"Rules that are compromised open the door to chaos," Mr. Trinidad sighed. "At least that's what the old Royal Council once believed."

"That's just down-to-the-bone dumb," I said.

Mr. Trinidad shrugged his shoulders and said, "We adults are often the biggest of boneheads, I'm afraid."

"Did you know my mother?"

"If it were not for your mother," he said, "you would be having this conversation with someone else. I probably would have had every ounce of my enchanted essence—my mythaloricals—drained out of my body by the Purifiers on some dreadful mining planet solely for the purpose of expanding their realm of power. Your mother saved my life. Spirited me away to this small blue planet called Earth. Trusted me to protect the other Sky Conjurers living on Earth. I watch the skies for them. That is why I am one of only twelve Sentinels stationed on this planet."

It was starting to sound like everybody knew my mother. Except me. Her daughter.

I'd never even seen a picture of her.

Everyone else had a picture of her in their memories. They could see her smile in their minds. Their hearts. They knew the color of her eyes and maybe even the way her skin and hair smelled.

I had grown up believing my mom and dad died in a car accident just after I was born. Aunt Monique and Uncle Joshua told me winter storm winds had blown their car off the Giovanni Angelo Bridge and into the East River. The car was pulled from the water the next spring. They never found my parents' bodies.

This was the story I was told, and not very often.

Enough years passed by where I didn't even want to hear the story again. It hurt too much.

Uncle Joshua and Aunt Monique became my parents. My mom and dad. They were my family. They were all I needed. All I wanted.

I didn't really think much about who my father was. Uncle Joshua once told me my father had been in the army. That he was a good man. I didn't ask much about him because whenever I did, I could see that it kind of hurt Uncle Joshua to talk about him. And besides, Uncle Joshua loved me and made me laugh and protected me and helped me with my homework and took me to gymnastics. If that's not being a father, girlfriend, I don't know what is.

Aunt Monique had always been like a mother to me. But there was still this hole in my heart where my for-real mother should have been.

The hole got bigger every year I got older.

"Who is Morabeau?" I asked.

"He was once a great and honorable Ashanti Kai Knight, like Joshua," Mr. Trinidad said, a tiny meteor whizzing over his left shoulder. "The Ashanti Kai are special warriors. They give up their birth names when they are trained as Ashanti Kai Knights. They are known only as 'The Body.' The Body protects the royal family. And they protect Sky Conjuring People too weak to defend themselves. They move in shadow so that others may live in the light. Unfortunately, Morabeau came to resent being nameless and having to live in the shadows. He found humans weak and petty, easily led and easily frightened like sheep. He finally used his conjuring powers and training to masquerade as a human, acquiring riches and fame that the humans seem to worship above all else. But I suspect his wealth has become a bit boring for him. It's power that he wants. Power beyond what this Earth can offer."

"I'm—I'm scared," I said.

"May I tell you a story, your Highness?" Mr. Trinidad asked.

His story began with a lion that was out hunting on a hot African afternoon. The lion saw a goat lying on top of a big rock. The goat was chewing slowly— "as goats often do even when they're not chewing anything at all!" Mr. Trinidad said. The lion crept up real close and was ready to make a hot lunch out of the goat. At the last minute the goat saw the lion, but instead of running, the goat kept on slowly chewing.

"Well, now, the lion—since he's hungry—he starts wondering what that goat's chewing on," Mr. Trinidad said. "See, there wasn't anything around except that big ol' rock. The lion, he gets up real close to the goat—so close the goat can feel the lion's hot breath on his neck and smell how bad the lion's breath is. The lion with a voice like thunder roars, 'Hey, goat! Wha'chu chewin' on?' Well, now, the goat was really, truly scared. But he just turned his head nice and slow, looked at that old lion right dead in his evil yellow eye and said, 'I'm chewin' on this here rock—and if you don't be gone when I'm through eatin' this rock, I'mo eat you!' Well, the lion does some quick calculating and finally figures, 'If that goat can chew on a rock and not bust a tooth, what can he do to me?' Well, the lion, scared of how his bones might sound crunchin' in the goat's mouth, cut and run as fast and as far as he could from that goat!"

When Mr. Trinidad finished his story, he was looking at me with a big, toothy grin peeking through his long, gray-bearded face.

"That's it?" I said.

"That's it," he said.

"Okay, so like, uh—what's the point?"

Mr. Trinidad brought his face closer to mine. He winked and said, "The point is, it's okay to be scared, your Highness. But a brave person will always find a way to defeat their fears. And in you, I see great bravery."

"I hope you're right," I said.

"So do I," Mr. Trinidad said grinning. "Because if I'm wrong, it would seem we're all pretty much badly hosed."

ENTRY SIX:

Run

The story Mr. Trinidad told me about the lion and the goat made me feel a little less scared. To be for real, girlfriend, I would have felt a whole lot better if his left eye hadn't started flashing red and yellow.

I stared at him with my mouth hung open, trying to find the words to tell him that his eye was doing a *bling-bling* thing.

As I stared at Mr. Trinidad's flashing eye, a southern woman's brown-sugar-and-molasses voice echoed throughout the room: "Proximity alert. Proximity alert. Y'all best be havin' a look-see."

Mr. Trinidad saw me staring at him.

"It's the eye thing, isn't it?" he asked, a little embarrassed.

I nodded slowly.

"Give it time," he said. "You'll get used to it ..."

I nodded, doubting I'd ever get used it.

We walked quickly toward Miss Lettie.

"You're not a—robot, are you?" I asked Mr. Trinidad.

"Oh, my heavens no," he said. "I lost my eye escaping from Hunters some years back. Eyes aren't something most conjurers can replace with a healing spell. Queen Yolanda—your mother—fixed me up with a bio-cybic eye. Part real eye, part nanometric, self-realizing, self-calibrating computer graphics, cortical systems interface."

I didn't ask.

"What's going on?" Aunt Monique asked as Mr. Trinidad and I passed her.

"Smell dat?" Miss Lettie asked, sniffing the air.

"I don't smell anything," I said.

But I did.

The air smelled a little like—black licorice.

Mr. Trinidad quickly held up his right hand and all the stars, all the planets and meteors in the room rushed back into a small blue and orange ball at the center of his palm before completely disappearing.

Another large image filled the room: three men in a boat with a big fan attached to the back. An airboat. I'd seen pictures of men using this kind of boat on the sluggish waters of the bayou and the Florida Everglades.

"Seems our Hunter friend didn't waste any time," Mr. Trinidad said, touching a floating computer screen. Symbols and numbers flashed on the screen. "Whoever used the Sentinel outposts to send that signal has really stirred the pot."

Two of the men in the boat were white. They looked like the kind of men black people grow up hearing boogeyman stories about: not too bright, not too nice, and full of pork ribs and beer. The other man was black and looked like the kind of man white people grow up hearing boogeyman stories about: not too bright, not too nice, and full of pork ribs and beer.

The men were drifting down the bayou river in their big airboat, not looking very concerned about much of anything. Maybe the heat was getting to them before they could drop their fishing lines in the muddy water. Maybe they were just being super-secret about trying to illegally hook an alligator.

Maybe they were just stupid and full of pork ribs and beer.

Looking at their droopy eyes and slack jaws, that would have been my guess.

"They're just fishing," I said. "See? Look at their fishing poles."

"Look again, your Highness," Miss Lettie said. "Dem poles way too short for fishin'. Dem's—"

"Spirit Wands!" Mr. Trinidad said.

The image quickly flickered off. "Hurry! Please hurry!" Mr. Trinidad shouted as he ran toward an unseen exit. "You must leave now!"

"What's going on?" I yelled, running alongside Aunt Monique.

"Bokubans!" she said.

"False creatures," Miss Lettie said, joining us. "Hunters manufacture Bokubans and use dem as trackers on planets where dey tink Sky Conjurers might be hidden. Dey smell like black licorice."

"Think of a rottweiller dog," Mr. Trinidad said, leaping through a round door. "Only half as bright, not nearly as nice, and with an even worse drooling problem."

We quickly followed Mr. Trinidad into a small room filled with bright, strange machines. He jumped into a silver chair that floated back and forth between the shining machines and flickering screens. The screens flashed different symbols and numbers and images of the Bokubans on the airboat.

"Bokubans identified," the unseen southern woman's voice said. "Two hundred yards from Sentinel outpost and closing."

"Three of them," Mr. Trinidad said, stroking his long white beard. "Okay, so the good news is no Hunter is holding their leash. The bad news is Bokubans usually track in pairs. Three means they're very, very serious about finding the queen. The *really* awful news is those are Series-5 Spirit Wands. Very bad. Explode every mythaloric cell in a conjurer's body from seventy-five yards away. And I think they have our scent."

I looked at one of the screens showing the Bokubans; their heads were arched back and they were sniffing the air. I mean *really* sniffing the air! Their nostrils expanded to half the size of their stupid faces!

"We must leave now," Miss Lettie said.

"Leave?" Aunt Monique said. "Are you crazy, old woman? The only place safer than St. Hestia is a Sentinel outpost. And besides— there isn't a slipstream gateway for at least two miles through this miserable swampland."

"Miss Lettie's right I'm afraid, Princess," said Mr. Trinidad. "You must leave. There are some very powerful spells and truly amazing technology protecting this outpost. But if you stay here we may lose control of this and every outpost on Earth. And that could compromise every Sky Conjurer on Earth. It might even endanger the humans."

"You and de girl make a run for it," Miss Lettie said. "I'll hold dem Bokubans off."

"You're not strong enough yet," Aunt Monique said. "And forgive me for saying, Miss Lettie, but I don't completely trust your abilities to protect anyone. You failed my sister. I will not have you fail Charlemagne."

"Ladies? Please?" Mr. Trinidad said nervously. "The Bokubans definitely have our scent. They are at one hundred yards and closing in on us quickly."

I looked at one of the silvery round screens: the three men had jumped off the boat and into the shallow black water. They reached the shore and began running through the thicket of trees and scrub bushes, sniffing the air like half-starved-and-all-crazy hunting dogs.

"I will not fail you, my Princess," Miss Lettie said, bowing her head and crossing her arms over her chest.

"You'd better not, old woman," Aunt Monique said. "Or you and I will settle our differences during a Breathing Time."

I gave Mr. Trinidad a quick kiss on his hairy cheek. I think I surprised him.

He bowed low to me and said, "Your time has come, your Highness."

"My time?" I said.

Mr. Trinidad rose from his bow, smiled at me, and said, "To believe in things larger than yourself."

"Be the goat," I said.

He winked at me and said, "Be the goat."

"Hurry!" Aunt Monique shouted.

We ran.

Back in the sticky heat of the bayou, the Bokubans quickly picked up full noses of our scent. Through the trees, they fired their black Spirit Wands. Bursts of white light exploded against trees in their path. I followed Aunt Monique. Miss Lettie ran behind me.

"Go! Go, go, *go!*" Miss Lettie shouted.

I looked back.

Miss Lettie jumped high into the air, spinning through the tangled tree limbs. She landed on one knee, her other leg stretched to her side. Not bad for a woman who had to be at *least* forty years old.

From the palms of her hands, two blinding bolts of lightning shot out toward the Bokubans. One of the lightning bolts hit a Bokuban in the chest and lifted it off its feet. Spinning in the air, it instantly changed from a human look-alike to a big bubbling ball of melting brown wax. It splattered on the ground, a lifeless blob.

"Hurry, Charlemagne!" Aunt Monique shouted.

Burning light from another Spirit Wand slammed into a small tree only a few feet in front of Aunt Monique. She stopped and turned on her heels.

"Get behind me!" she yelled.

The Bokuban stretched his Spirit Wand out at us.

Aunt Monique leaped into the air and began spinning with her arms out to her sides. Leaves, dirt, and old fallen tree limbs whirled up into the air like a small, dirty tornado.

The tornado bounced off the ground a couple of times before hitting the Bokuban, lifting him into the air and flipping him around like a seriously out of control pop-and-lock break-dancer.

Aunt Monique stopped spinning. From her hands she threw two balls of orange light at the spinning Bokuban.

Direct hit.

The smell of burning black licorice.

Dark brown wax slapped against the side of a tree and dripped in heavy, lifeless globs onto the ground below.

"Since when can you do *that*?" I asked as she landed.

Two Bokubans down, one to go.

"You are the Orisha!" a deep voice growled. The third Bokuban.

I looked over my shoulder.

He was gaining on us, running in big leaps, the nostrils of his nose blown up like balloons and filled with our scent.

Miss Lettie was nowhere in sight.

Maybe Aunt Monique was right about her. Maybe she had let my mother down when my mother had needed her the most.

I shouldn't have looked back. I tripped over a rotting log and fell head over heels onto the damp ground. The Bokuban stood over me, pointing his Spirit Wand at my head.

"You are the Orisha," it said, in a voice that sounded like it was gargling snot.

"Charlemagne!"

It was my aunt.

The Bokuban brought his Spirit Wand up and fired a white bolt of lightning at her. She dropped, rolled, and came up to her knees. But before she could do anything the Bokuban fired again. This time the lightning bolt missed her and exploded against the tree next to her. The tree fell on her leg and there was an awful cracking sound.

Aunt Monique screamed in pain.

"No!" I shouted at the Bokuban.

I was scared and crying.

I raised the palm of my left hand. Yellow light crackled out of my hand and hit the Bokuban in the chest. It knocked him back several feet.

"You... are... the Orisha," it said, stumbling toward me again, dark brown wax bubbling from its chest.

"No!" I shouted again, sending another stream of yellow light out toward him. "No! No! No!"

It kept coming at me.

"When da queen say no," I heard Miss Lettie say, "she mean no."

The Bokuban turned to face her. She looked weak and was barely able to stand, but she let loose with two bolts of white light from her hands. The light spun around the Bokuban. The Bokuban began shaking uncontrollably.

But it wasn't enough.

The light storm around the Bokuban faded and it stepped through the remaining sparkles of light. It pointed its Spirit Wand at me.

Miss Lettie dropped to her knees, exhausted.

All I could do was watch the Bokuban stumble toward me, stinking brown wax bubbling from its chest.

Suddenly, a bolt of yellow light hit the Bokuban. It lifted it off his feet and slammed it into a tree less than five feet away from me.

A splash of warm, dark wax hit my face.

Miss Lettie made her way to me.

"Thank you," I said.

She was exhausted and blood was trickling down her cheek. "It wasn't me, girl-girl. And it wasn't your aunt."

"Mr. Trinidad?" I said.

Miss Lettie shook her head no. Her eyes darted around, searching the thick forest. Under her breath she whispered, "Morabeau."

Miss Lettie helped me to my feet and we ran to Aunt Monique's side. Her right leg was pinned beneath a heavy tree limb.

Her leg was broken.

Miss Lettie used her remaining strength to lift the log off of Aunt Monique's leg.

"Go," my aunt said through her pain. Seeing her lying there with a broken leg hurt me all the way through to my soul.

"I can heal you," Miss Lettie said.

"You're weak, old woman," she said. "Besides, someone has to stay behind to clean up any traces of the Bokubans. Leave me. I can heal this leg. Go."

"What about me?" I said. "I healed Miss Lettie. I'm sure I can—"

"Your powers are great, Charlemagne," my aunt said. "But you're still untrained. You could do more to hurt me than heal me."

"I won't leave you," I said crying.

"You must, Charlemagne," she said. "Like it or not, you are not a little girl any more. You are a queen. And that means you cannot just do what you feel like doing. You have to do what's right. Leaving me now is the right thing to do."

I looked up at Miss Lettie. She nodded her head, agreeing with my aunt.

"I'll be fine," Aunt Monique said. "I promise."

"De Sentinel will give her refuge for a while," Miss Lettie said.

"Go, Charlemagne," Aunt Monique said. "You must go now."

I hugged her.

I'd lost my mother a long time ago. I'd lost my uncle yesterday. The thought of losing my aunt over things I didn't understand made me feel very alone, very confused, and very, very scared. Aunt Monique had made me honey-lemon green tea when I was sick. Baked me chocolate chip cookies. She'd held me in her arms and sung songs to me that made my fears go away before I went to sleep.

"I love you," I said to her.

"I love you, too, Charley Mack."

"St. Hestia," Miss Lettie said to my aunt.

Aunt Monique nodded and said, "St. Hestia. Three days."

And then Miss Lettie and I ran, leaving my aunt behind in the miserable heat, in the dirt, and surrounded by the bubbling brown mess of the dead Bokubans.

"Keep her safe, old woman!" my aunt shouted through the trees. "If you don't, then you will fear me more than any Hunter!"

ENTRY SEVEN:

Ladies and Gentlmen! Mr. Robillard "Rib Sauce" Sheppard

I was somewhere between the land below and the moon above. Flying.

Miss Lettie was sailing through the air at my side, keeping me from bouncing off the freezing cold sides of the slipstream. According to Miss Lettie, it wasn't really bouncing off the sides of the slipstream that I had to worry about. It was falling out of the slipstream completely that I had to worry about. Most Sky Conjurers can fly on their own power up to about two or three hundred feet off the ground. Falling out of the slipstream meant a Sky Conjurer—even a good one—would fall fifteen miles before he could fire up his own magical flying power. And by then, he'd be frozen like one big ice cube.

And then... boom.

That wasn't no meteorite that just made a crater in the ground, girlfriend.

Even so, most conjurers choose the slipstream for travel.

It's faster and cheaper than the airlines. Satellites don't see us. And radar can't find us.

"You okay, girl-girl?" Miss Lettie said.

"A little cold," I said. "But, yeah, okay. You?"

"You saved my life, your Highness," she said. "Nobody ever been saved from a Dark Matter infection. I be forever in your debt."

I still wasn't sure I trusted Miss Lettie.

But for the moment, I didn't have much of a choice.

It's hard to tell time when you're riding the slipstream. We might have been flying for ten minutes. We could have been whirly-gigging and spinning for an hour. Time sort of loses its meaning when you're sailing on air between the stars above and the city lights below.

All I know is when Miss Lettie and I landed, it was night in New Orleans.

The streets and narrow sidewalks were crowded with people pushing and shoving past each other while kids my age and younger picked their pockets and ran away laughing.

"What are we doing here?" I asked Miss Lettie as we ducked and dodged our way through the crowds of people. I was holding on tight to Miss Lettie's arm, scared of getting separated from her in the crush of people on a street named Bourbon.

"Trust be de key to feelin' safe," Miss Lettie said as we made our way through the loud, annoying crowd. "I know I not be exactly trusted by you or da Princess. So I bring you to somebody you can trust wid your whole heart. A friend who be keepin' you safe."

I stopped and looked up at her.

"Those Bokubans," I said, suddenly feeling my whole body losing the battle against crying. "They were going to—hurt me."

"No," Miss Lettie said kneeling down and looking me straight in my eyes. "No, dey wasn't gonna hurt you, girl-girl. Dey be needin' you, your Highness."

"Need me?" I said. "For what?"

"Dey still do not have de Star Charm," she said. "And you be da key to finding it."

I lost the battle to hold back my tears. Even in the awful New Orleans heat, in the middle of a rude, sweaty, bumping, and pushing crowd, I felt myself shaking like I was freezing cold. "They want to hurt me over something I don't even know anything about."

"Shhh," Miss Lettie said. "Gonna be awright, Miss Charley Mack. I'll see to dat."

There were tears in her eyes, too.

I don't know why, but I wiped them away.

I think we were both feeling like we could use somebody we could trust.

"Girlfriends?" I said.

She looked at me stunned for a second, then smiled, nodded, and said, "Girlfriends."

We pushed and sidestepped our way through the crowd and into a small restaurant called Jimmy's House of Ju-Ju, where ceiling fans stirred up the stink of too many sweating people, too much grease burning, and way too much nasty cigarette smoke.

We pushed and shoved through the beer-drinking, cigarette-smoking crowd to the back of the restaurant. A sign posted outside of a small room read "Live Music Returns!"

We got there just in time to hear the last bit of whoever was on stage singing the blues:

I got myself a
Big Furry Bottom
And I got me a tail that wag all night long
Oh, honey, I got me a
Big Furry Bottom
And a tail that wag all night long
Furry Bottom Blues, baby
Is what make me to howl this here sad, sad song
Everybody!

People with huge glasses of glow-in-the-dark drinks pushed out of the room and past us.

"What the heck was *that* guy all about?" a man said to his girlfriend, who was teetering back and forth unsteadily on high heels.

"I don't know," his girlfriend said, giggling. "I thought he was kind of cute. I liked the song about the dog with the furry butt."

A handmade sign just to the right of the music stage read: "Robillard 'Rib Sauce' Sheppard. New Orleans's Blues Man Extraordinaire." Underneath the headline was a smaller sentence that read, "And qualified Century 21 Real Estate Agent. Call …"

On the stage in front of ten small, round, and empty tables was a fat black man in a shiny purple three-piece suit with a pink shirt, yellow silk tie, and white straw hat.

Just when I was getting used to Sky Conjurers not having any money, they just *had* to go and show me how embarrassingly fashion-impaired they were.

"Where'd you learn to play, man?" somebody called out from the exit.

Mr. Robillard "Rib Sauce" Sheppard was now polishing his shiny red electric guitar. The fat blues man grinned, shrugged, and said, "Oh, hey man, you know—I just picked it up."

"Yeah, well, maybe you should throw it back," the man said before pushing his way past us, grumbling something about how Hurricane Katrina had washed away all the *real* New Orleans talent.

The man on the stage saw Miss Lettie and me standing by the door. His eyes widened and he stopped polishing his guitar.

His eyes darted around the room nervously, then back to us.

Slowly, he put his guitar in a stand, mopped his sweating forehead with the same handkerchief he'd polished his guitar with, and announced to the empty room, "Well, tha's it for tonight, y'all. I be back tomorrow night. Same tardy time, same funky place for your live Delta blues music entertainment. I'm Robillard 'Rib Sauce' Sheppard. Eat well and tip generously, ya hear?"

Then with a quick jerk of his round head, he gestured for Miss Lettie and me to follow him.

In a small office at the back of the restaurant, Mr. Sheppard crossed his arms over his chest and bowed deeply to Miss Lettie and me. Before I knew what was going on, he had dropped to his knees, grabbed both of my hands, then began licking them and crying like a baby with a bad case of gas.

"You better *step* off, chump!" I shouted, trying to yank my hands away from this fat slobbering fool. I finally pulled my hands free and wiped his slobber on my really dirty pajamas.

"It be all right, your Highness" Miss Lettie said. "He just a little overcome wid emotion is all—"

"This dude's gonna be my *bodyguard*?" I shouted. "N'uh uh! No, I don't think so! And look at that suit! Don't you think whoever's after me will kind of *see* that suit?"

Mr. Sheppard whimpered, "Your Highness, your blessed royal Highness..."

Miss Lettie put a hand gently on Mr. Sheppard's shoulder. "Mr. Sheppard. Please. Dat be enough."

"Forgive me," he said standing and hanging his head low. "I have dishonored myself with such a display. Completely unprofessional."

"You ain't lyin'," I said wondering if all Star Conjurers were just really weird losers.

"Mr. Sheppard," Miss Lettie said. "Your special services be very much needed again."

"I am without reservation or hesitation humbly at your service," Mr. Sheppard said with another bow.

Okay, so like, sometimes just when you think things can't possibly get any worse, they do, right? Well, by this time I'd had a big, bad belly full of the whole Bad-To-Worse thing. I didn't care about being a queen or having magical, mystical super-witch powers or having ultra-weird nutcases call me "your Highness." Right now, all I wanted was a shower so I didn't smell like a boy, a medium veggie pizza (no mushrooms), and to wake up from this awful nightmare in my own bed at my old apartment.

But no.

Instead of chillin' out in front of BET, Discovery Channel, or Animal Planet, it was midnight and I was walking through a New Orleans graveyard with some old-as-dirt island witch-woman dressed like a back-in-the-day hippie chick and an overweight black man dressed like some neon-retro Super Fly Mack Daddy.

I was seriously beginning to miss math quizzes and lukewarm 800-miligrams-of-sodium school lunches.

Even gym class with LaZonia Johnson was starting to look pretty good.

ENTRY EIGHT:

Sweet Home, Nappy Valley

I had hoped the graveyard was just a shortcut to Mr. Sheppard's house.

But no.

That would've been too normal.

Mr. Sheppard actually lived *in* one of the graves.

Not exactly where you'd expect a Century 21 real estate agent to live. But then he was also a New Orleans blues singer, so I figured he must have had a whole lot of serious emotional baggage going on.

Frankly, I didn't know what his gig was.

And girlfriend, I *really* didn't care.

All I knew was a tall stone grave slab slid open and Mr. Sheppard started to walk down into the grave. I turned to Miss Lettie and said, "Oh, *heck* no, lady! You are out of your dang mind if you think I'm walking down into a *grave!*"

"It be all right, your Highness," she said.

"No, see, like, what part of *out of your dang mind* don't you understand?" I said. "Let me hit REPLAY for you. I'm twelve years old and we are following a brotha dressed for Halloween at the Apollo Theater into some creepy New Orleans grave! AT MIDNIGHT! Don't y'all people live nowhere *close* to normal? Apartments? Adobes? Houses? Tents? Teepees?"

Miss Lettie gently placed her fingertips on my forehead. I felt my body go limp. I still knew what was going on and I was still freaking out inside, but my entire body felt light. Like I was floating.

Which I was.

Floating through the narrow marble door of the grave, over steps leading down into the dark, cold grave.

There was the awful sound of the stone door of the grave grinding closed behind us. I was floating through the darkness. I couldn't move my arms or legs. I couldn't scream. All I could do was wish my life had been different; I wished I had lived in a neighborhood where people were actually neighbors. I wished I had friends that laughed and played with me. I wished I hadn't stopped talking to my mother in my dreams.

And right about now I seriously I wished I'd gone to church more often.

A light snapped on.

I expected to see evil-looking, evil-smelling zombies with green skin and oozing scabs dressed in last year's Tommy Hilfiger jeans and Air Jordan basketball shoes.

No zombies.

No vampires.

Instead, we were in a nice living room with comfortable furniture, lots of books, a CD player, and bunches of posters of blues singers on the walls.

Miss Lettie released my body from her spell.

"Don't you *ever, never* do that to me again, lady!" I shouted.

"Forgive me, your Highness," Miss Lettie said hanging her head down.

I didn't say anything else.

"Welcome to my modest home, your Highness," Mr. Sheppard said. "Can I get you something? Water? Juice? I'm afraid I haven't been conjuring food much lately, so the cupboard's a bit bare. I could whip up a nice Altarian lemon-and-blue-olive-custard sponge cake if you'd like."

"Pass," I said hoping Sky Conjurers didn't eat as poorly as they dressed.

"Not much time," Miss Lettie said, sitting on the sofa and rubbing the arm where her wound had been. "Three Bokubans tracked us to de Sentinel. Dey know Miss Charlemagne be da new Queen of Sky Conjurers. But dey don't know where Queen Yolanda hid de Star Charm. Dey tink Miss Charlemagne can lead dem to it."

Mr. Sheppard nodded, then slowly began walking in circles. After a while, he walked to a large floor pillow in a corner of the room and lay on it. He was deep in thought. I kind of wish he'd given his suit as much thought.

After a few minutes, Mr. Sheppard looked up at Miss Lettie and said, "How much have you taught her?"

"Been no time, old friend," she said. "But her powers be great. Perhaps de most powerful I seen in 263 years."

"Say *what*?" I said cutting Miss Lettie a look. "Exactly how old are you, lady?"

"Dis October, I be 298 Earth years, your Highness."

"Oh, dang, girl," I said. "I mean, for real—you look *good* for being, like, older than Madonna."

Miss Lettie shrugged. "I moisturize. Watch what I eat. No refined sugar. No pork. And I stopped eating Volarian slug fish eighty-five years ago."

"Oh," I said not wanting to think about what a Volarian slug fish might look like. "Good for you."

"Does Princess Monique know you're here?" Mr. Sheppard asked.

"No," Miss Lettie said. "She will meet us on St. Hestia in three days."

"Good," Mr. Sheppard said with a quick nod. "I would suggest we be on the island in two. And what about Morabeau? Is he involved in any of this?"

"Don't know," Miss Lettie said. "But I feel his shadow be on dis situation in some way."

"I hope so," Mr. Sheppard said with a strange growl. "I'd like to settle a few things with that rotten son of a ..." He looked at me and fell silent.

Mr. Sheppard was quiet for another minute. Then he said, "I'll agree to serve the queen on one condition."

"And dat be?"

"No restrictions this time," he said. "I must be allowed to return to my own true Altarian form even among the humans. You can't believe how much this suit itches."

"Well, of course it does, brotha," I said. "That's 100 percent old-school polyester! You lucky you ain't all fallin' out in hives."

"I agree to your terms," Miss Lettie said to Mr. Sheppard. "Dey be my terms as well."

Mr. Sheppard sighed, then said, "We have to see the Oracle of the Bluffs. We'll leave in the morning. Until then, please make yourself comfortable, your Highness."

I asked Miss Lettie if she could conjure up a spell for a large veggie pizza (no mushrooms), a stack of chili fries, large bag of Cheetos, and a frosty bottle of Cherry Vanilla Snazzle Razz soda.

She did.

I hate to admit it, but I ate like a boy. All elbows, grunts, and too much food in my mouth at one time. I couldn't remember the last time I'd eaten. And not knowing when—or if—I'd ever eat again, I for sure dived mouth-first into this little feast.

"One of da first things I must teach you," Miss Lettie said, her face all twisted up in disgust as she watched me eat, "is proper diet and table manners for a queen."

"Lady," I said with my mouth full, "You say 'tink' instead of 'think' and 'dey' instead of 'they.' How you gonna teach me how to be a queen?"

Miss Lettie looked a little hurt when I said that.

"It might better serve her Highness," she said with her head lowered, "to pay attention to de soul of my words instead of de color of my accent."

Eating wasn't the only thing I was doing like a boy. Halfway through the pizza I caught a whiff of myself. Running through the Louisiana heat and sweating like a pig made me smell nasty like a boy, too. I was full and exhausted by the time I finished the pizza. Now all I wanted was a nice, hot shower, and to go to sleep and wake up in time to go school. It was way past time for this nightmare to be over, girl.

I hadn't closed the bathroom door all the way when I heard Mr. Sheppard and Miss Lettie whispering.

"She must never be out of our sight," Miss Lettie said. "Not for a minute. Not for a single second."

"And the Princess?"

"She is not a concern now," Miss Lettie said.

"Oh, but she *will* be a concern very soon," Mr. Sheppard said. "It happened the last time, and you and I have suffered greatly for it."

"Our suffering ends with dis one," Miss Lettie said, nodding toward the bathroom door.

I quietly closed the door of the small bathroom, got in the shower, and cried.

After my shower, I slipped into a fresh pair of white cotton pajamas and a purple silk robe Miss Lettie had conjured up for me. She was sitting on the sofa in the living room and feeding a slice of leftover pizza to a scruffy-looking dog with long ears and brown spots. The dog's tail wagged happily as he munched on the pizza and begged for more.

"Is this Mr. Sheppard's dog?" I asked, trying to act like everything was cool. Which it wasn't.

"No," Miss Lettie said, smiling.

The dog suddenly stood on his hind legs, bowed at the waist, and said, "Your Highness."

Screaming, I fell backward into a chair and against something squishy. Whatever it was wheezed an asthmatic sigh and made a weird accordion sound.

I jumped up, turned, and looked at the squishy thing in the chair: it was a rubbery-looking human body. The lifeless body of the man I knew as Robillard "Rib Sauce" Sheppard.

I screamed again and fell backward on the sofa next to Miss Lettie.

"It's a suit, your Highness," Mr. Sheppard the dog said. "Just a suit. Well, actually it's an older TK-3 Bio-cybic Human Suit. Not very comfortable, and they still hadn't quite worked out how to make the thumbs work properly. Probably why my guitar playing has suffered."

"You're—you're a dog," I said, feeling my heart pounding hard against my chest.

"An Altarian actually," the dog said. "Admittedly, there are physical similarities between Altarians and the earth canine species. Just as there are similarities between today's humans and their hairy, slack-jawed, and none-too-bright evolutionary ancestors of 40,000 years ago."

"You're—a *dog*," I repeated, not believing I was speaking to a dog who was speaking to me.

"This is going to take some time, isn't it," he said.

Okay, so there I was; down in some cold, damp New Orleans grave with an elderly hippie witch-woman, a talking dog, and a rubber suit of a fat man in purple jacket and pants. And let's not forget there were some very bad alien-type people out there hunting for me.

Great recipe for a nice night's sleep, huh?

Nighty-noodles …

The next morning the three of us—Mr. Sheppard, Miss Lettie, and me—left New Orleans on a slipstream heading east.

When we spun out of the slipstream we found ourselves bunched tightly together inside a small, dark room that smelled like old wood, cotton candy, and stale popcorn.

Miss Lettie opened the door of the small wooden room and we walked out into the bright, hot sunshine.

We had landed inside the most beautiful carousel I'd ever seen! At least twenty or thirty hand-carved, hand-painted horses on shiny brass poles. And there were rings of brightly colored lights hung all the way around the carousel.

"Where are we?" I asked Miss Lettie.

"Oak Bluff, Massachusetts," Miss Lettie said. "On an island called Martha's Vineyard."

It was warm, but not like New Orleans.

Saltwater breezes drifted in off the Atlantic Ocean, taking the midday sting out of the sun's bright rays.

"The Oracle's this way," Mr. Sheppard said, sniffing the air before trotting off on all fours.

"You know he's a dog, right?" I said to Miss Lettie.

She smiled at me, and then we followed Mr. Sheppard until we were at a large white house with green shutters and a screened-in porch that faced out to the tan beach and blue ocean. Hanging next to the screen door of the porch was a cheap little plastic sign that read, "Gardening Grows On You." Hanging from the white porch ceiling were all kinds of wind chimes catching the soft breezes off the ocean. And there were all kinds of plants growing out of a bright, colorful assortment of pots.

But most of all, there was the smell of pie.

Warm, freshly baked apple pie with cinnamon.

An old woman's high, creaky voice came from inside the house. "Come on in, y'all! Come on in! Felt you coming on the slipstream, so I baked us a pie. You like apple pie don't you, Miss Charlemagne?"

Miss Lettie opened the screen door and we all stepped onto the porch. I was hoping—praying!—this old lady didn't look like a spider the size of a farm animal.

"Yes, ma'am," I said nervously, looking around at everything on the porch. "I like apple pie."

"Well, honey," the woman said with her skritchy-scratchy voice, "let's eat us some."

The old woman walked onto the porch carrying the biggest, lumpiest, most delicious-smelling apple-cinnamon pie I'd ever seen.

The old woman couldn't have been any taller than me. And if Miss Lettie was 287 years old, then this wrinkled prune of a black lady had to be at *least* 600! She wore black linen chimney slacks, black stretch fabric sandals, a white linen blouse, and a rose-colored cotton sweater casually draped over her slumped shoulders.

Finally!

A conjurer with fashion sense!

"Sister-woman," the old black woman said, giving Miss Lettie a gentle hug and pat on her back.

"Sister-woman," Miss Lettie said, returning the hug.

"And you, you old coot," the woman said, crouching and scratching Mr. Sheppard behind his ears. "Been a long time, hasn't it, Mr. Sheppard?"

"A long time," Mr. Sheppard said, enjoying being scratched behind his floppy ears.

Then the old woman turned and looked at me.

Her eyes were milky white.

She was blind.

"Miss Charlemagne Althea Mack," she sighed. "Your coming was foretold by the *Book of Legends*. Would you follow me, please? I need you to pick out what kind of ice cream you'd like with your pie."

We walked through her house toward the kitchen. Inside, the house was crowded with old-looking African drums and scary-looking African masks. Pictures of people hung all over the walls, floor to ceiling. All kinds of people. Black and white and Mexican and Chinese and East Indians. And there were all kinds of rugs and sculptures and artwork strewn about on the floor and any remaining wall space.

"I just picked up three quarts of ice cream from Mad Martha's Ice Cream Parlor," the old woman said. "Choco Chunk Cherry, Vanilla Fudge Typhoon, and Pistachio Cream Soda. Which one would you like, dear? Maybe a scoop of all three?"

"You're blind," I heard myself say.

Oops.

My bad.

The old woman's white eyes fixed on me. She smiled. Even though she was blind it felt like she was staring right to the center of my soul.

"Oh, it's true I can no longer use these eyes to see, if that's what you mean," she said pointing to the white marbles of her eyes with a finger that looked like the withered tree branch. "But what I see through sound and taste and smell and touch and spirit shows me so much more than my eyes ever did. What you see with your eyes can often be more deceiving than what you feel with your heart, dear."

"I thought conjurers lost their magical powers without their eyes," I said. "At least that's what Mr. Trinidad told me."

"Ah, Mr. Trinidad!" she said laughing. "And how is my favorite Sentinel?"

"Fine," I said with a shrug. "I guess."

"He sent me an e-mail last Christmas," she said. "Goodness knows I had a hard time explaining to my neighbors what an elephant was doing in my front yard."

"How do you—"

"Well, I can't drive a car if that's where you're going with your question, dear," she said. "Wouldn't want to anyway. Awful, smelly things without the slightest bit of poetry to them. But what I have lost through sight has only given me greater gifts of spirit."

"I think I'll have the Pistachio Cream Soda ice cream, please," I said.

"Excellent choice!"

"You already knew what kind of ice cream I was going to choose, didn't you?" I said. "I mean that's why they call you the Oracle, right? You see the future. You read people's minds."

She pulled the quart of Pistachio Cream Soda ice cream out of the freezer and said, "Oh, honey, I stopped reading people's minds three hundred years ago, when I discovered most people were thinking about very little other than themselves."

"What's your name?" I said. "I mean your real name. I feel kind of funny calling you 'The Oracle.' Sounds like a DJ, not a name."

She smiled at me, handed me a bowl of Pistachio Cream Soda ice cream and said, "Why don't you just call me Miss Evelyn."

She started to walk away.

"Miss Evelyn?" I said.

"You're going to ask me if I trust Miss Lettie and Mr. Sheppard," she said with her back to me. "You're scared of them. You don't quite know if you can trust them. And for some strange reason something in your heart says you can trust me. Is that about right, dear?"

"Yes, ma'am. That's about right," I said.

"Reading minds is one thing," she laughed. "Hearing the beat and feeling the rhythm of someone else's heart is another." She turned and gently touched my arm. "Without the protection of Miss Lettie and Mr. Sheppard, your life in this world will end, leaving the prophecies of the *Book of Legends* unfulfilled for another thousand years," she said. "Miss Lettie and Mr. Sheppard both have secrets. Secrets that can only be revealed in time by them."

"One more question, Miss Evelyn?" I said.

"Of course," she said. "You may ask me anything you wish, your Highness."

"I don't mean to get all up in your business, but—uh—just how old are you?"

"I lost count at about 680 Earth years," she said smiling. "I still get birthday cards. Most folk just pick a date on a calendar and send me a card every year on that date. You can do the same if you want, your Highness."

"Must be kinda cool living that long," I said.

"Oh, I don't know," she said, "You see, I've always believed that it's not how long you live, but how generously you've given of your life. Does that make sense to you, dear?"

"Yeah—yes, ma'am," I said with a shrug. "I guess." We both stood facing each other for a few seconds more. She knew what I was going to ask, but she waited for me to ask anyway.

I cleared my throat, swallowed hard and said, "How old am I—I mean really?"

"You, my dear," she said smiling, "are twelve years old."

After we ate the apple-cinnamon pie and ice cream, Miss Evelyn showed me to the bedroom where I was to sleep until it was time for something called the Breathing Time. The room was all white-and cream-colored lace and had a four-poster bed draped in twirls of white chiffon. It looked like the kind of bedroom where only good dreams were allowed.

Miss Evelyn laid out a pair of white cotton pajamas for me. I put them on and climbed into the big, soft bed.

"The Breathing Time ritual is short," Miss Evelyn said. "But you must be well rested for it."

"You're not gonna, like, cut off some chicken's head, are you?" I said. "Or hang a black cat upside down over my heart? 'Cause, if that's what this Breathing Time ritual thing is all about, you can forget it."

"No," Miss Evelyn laughed. "There will be none of that. You'll be fine, I promise. Now you should get some sleep, your Highness."

Just as I was about to drift off to sleep, I heard them talking on the porch. They were trying to whisper, but I could still hear them.

"You know I can't do that, Miss Lettie," Miss Evelyn said. "All Sky Conjurers are welcomed here. Even him. If he requests my guidance in the Breathing Time ritual, then he will receive it."

"Then you must at least delay him," Mr. Sheppard said. "There's nothing that says an Oracle can't hold ceremony up a bit, right?"

"Perhaps I can delay him," Miss Evelyn said. "But be warned. Alidus Morabeau may be the danger that is walking your way. But he does not walk alone ..."

72

★

ENTRY NINE:

The Key

An hour?

Five hours?

I don't know how long I slept, but the touch of Miss Evelyn's warm hand on my cheek woke me up.

"It's time, your Highness," she said.

She was standing over me. In the darkness of the room I could see her blind white eyes glowing.

I don't know why, but I didn't freak out. I wasn't scared. In fact, with her glowing white eyes, Miss Evelyn looked like an angel.

Okay, a really *old* angel, but an angel just the same.

In her right hand she held on to a tall wooden walking stick draped with yellow straw and long green grass woven around it. There were all kinds of shiny beads wrapped around the middle of the stick. On top of the stick was a carved wooden African mask with large eyes that were closed.

Another set of clothes was laid out for me at the end of the bed—a purple silk gown and floor-length white silk vest. I put them on and followed Miss Evelyn downstairs and out of the house toward the beach.

As we walked, she explained the secret of mythaloricals to me, which goes something like this...

Ever feel like someone's behind you staring and you turn around and there they are—staring right at you?

Or maybe you've been thinking a lot about a friend, and suddenly the phone rings and you pick it up and your friend is on the other end of the line?

Mythaloricals.

Invisible cells in your blood, in your muscles and bones that give your mind, body, and spirit the ability to reach out and feel what you thought couldn't be felt. Mythaloricals let you see what's hidden from your eyes but not from your mind and heart. They're passed down from family member to family member, child to child. They hold the memories and hopes of ancestors. And they help guide children that haven't even been born.

Miss Evelyn says even humans have mythalorical cells. Cells that can give them an enchanted and magical life.

But most people tune them out or turn them off by not believing in such things as miracles and magic. Believing in a power that's bigger than the boredom you can see, taste, touch, hear, and smell is considered weird. Freaky. Unnatural.

Miss Evelyn says most people these days find it easier to believe in movie stars, DJs, MP3s, DVDs, and MTV.

Sky Conjurers have a high count of mythalorical cells in their blood. It's what gives them their powers. It's their link to their history, their culture, and souls past and yet to be born.

Oh, and by the way...

...sometimes mythaloricals can be programmed.

Which is why Miss Evelyn and Miss Lettie and Mr. Sheppard and I all stood on a dark, cold beach somewhere between twilight, night, and morning.

The Breathing Time.

A time when all the oceans around the world take a deep breath at the same time and exhale atoms of metals and minerals and secret light into the air. All of these things give more power to a conjurer's mythaloricals. Like magical Gatorade.

Miss Evelyn, Miss Lettie, and Mr. Sheppard were hoping the secret to where my mother had hidden the Star Charm would be unlocked in me through the Breathing Time ritual. They were hoping my mythaloricals would whisper secrets to me in my mother's voice.

So was I.

Kind of.

I mean how would I know it was my mother's voice? I'd never even *heard* her voice...

"Ready, your Highness?" Miss Evelyn said.

"No," I said. "Yes. I don't know."

Mr. Sheppard walked up to me on his hind legs. "Your Highness," he whispered. "Whatever you may think of me, I have sworn an oath to never let harm come to you. If you fear this ritual, I will not let it happen. However, the one thing you must never fear is to command me."

I nodded.

I looked at Miss Lettie.

She smiled and nodded at me.

I looked at Miss Evelyn and said, "Ain't nothin' to it but to do it, girl. Let's do this thang."

Miss Evelyn nodded, and then raised the tall stick with the African mask on it up to the deep purple sky.

"We greet you, Giver of Life, Goddess of All, with One Spirit and Many Strengths!" Miss Evelyn said. "Bring forth the Breathing Time and let us know who we, your children, truly are!"

Golden sparkles shimmered over the ocean and formed a constellation of bright yellow fireflies swooping and swirling and spiraling up toward the dark sky. As the flickers of light grew it looked like a meteor shower with millions of tiny meteors dancing everywhere.

Suddenly a stream of the bright yellow sparkles rushed toward us. I was scared, but I didn't move. Tell you the truth, girlfriend, I don't know if I could have moved even if I'd wanted to!

The stream of light slammed into the African mask Miss Evelyn held on top of her stick. Slowly, the mask's closed eyes and small wooden mouth opened wide, and bright white light shot out. The light hit me. It didn't hurt, but I felt my body jerk and I was lifted gently into the air. I tried to speak—to scream—but I couldn't. I was surrounded by thousands of flashing yellow and white lights. They danced around me, went through my skin, and raced out of my body.

Voices.

I heard voices.

Hundreds—maybe even thousands—of voices. Some of the voices were speaking strange languages. They all spoke at once, but it wasn't confusing to me. It was more like—music. Different notes that were building a song in me, through me, for me. I listened to all of them.

Then...

...one voice...

"You will always have my love, dear Charlemagne."

My mother.

The other voices faded into the background while my mother's voice rippled through me like cool, clean water.

I tried to speak to her, but I couldn't.

"It's time, my sweet baby girl," she said. "Know that I will always love you. Nothing will ever conquer that. You must trust your instincts. Your heart. Darkness is coming—and your strength must be the hammer that hits this darkness so that it bleeds light."

I don't remember much of anything after that.

When I woke up I was lying on the beach, my head cradled in Miss Lettie's lap. She was stroking my hair, my face, and she was humming what sounded like a lullaby.

There were tears in her eyes.

"You did this ritual for my mother, too, didn't you?" I said.

She nodded her head yes.

"She loved you very much," I said. "I could feel it."

Again, Miss Lettie nodded.

I sat up and looked into her eyes. "She still does," I said.

Miss Evelyn knelt in the sand next to Miss Lettie and me.

"Well," she said brightly. "I'd say that went quite well. How are you feeling, dear?"

"A little cold," I said. "And I can't move."

"Oh, you'll be just fine," she said. "Everybody feels like that the first time. A little rest, a little Moogoa-root tea with honey and lemon, and you'll be as good as new."

Mr. Sheppard stood at the edge of the beach, looking out over the ocean.

"Guard duty," Miss Lettie said.

I tried to look down at my body. I was stiff as a board. My right hand was balled up in a tight, shaking fist. I couldn't open my fist. I couldn't stop it from shaking.

After what seemed ages, my body relaxed and my fist stopped shaking. My fingers loosened and slowly opened. Something gold and flat was in the center of my hand.

Miss Evelyn squinted down at what I was holding. After a minute, her eyes widened. She stared at Miss Lettie and said, "Well! Well, well, well! It appears the key to finding the Star Charm is a library card."

⌀

ENTRY TEN:

"Yo! I come in peace..."

We stayed with Miss Evelyn until the next morning.

Mr. Sheppard woke me up.

"We must leave, your Highness," he said, standing on his hind legs at the end of my bed. The look in his big brown eyes told me it was time to go *now*.

Spinning through the slipstream, above the clouds and under the sun until we arrived...

...somewhere in the blue waters of the Atlantic Ocean. A place where books and *The Discovery Channel* say ships disappear and airplanes vanish. This is where compass dials spin around and around not knowing East from West, North from South.

The Bermuda Triangle.

And now I'll tell you what lives hidden in these mysterious blue ocean waters...

An island.

The most beautiful island you'll probably never see.

St. Hestia.

Only Sky Conjurers live here. The ones who don't live on the island come here for vacation. They come for the food and music, comfort and security. On St. Hestia, they don't have to pretend to be anybody or anything except who they really are.

Miss Lettie says when Sky Conjurers landed on Earth a thousand years ago, escaping from the Purifiers, they built this island from scratch. They hid it from humans through powerful spirits, spells, prayers, and technology. Great and powerful Sky Conjurers gave up every bit of their magical powers and wealth just to hide the island and its people from any Purifiers or Hunter Scouts who might wander into this forgotten little corner of the galaxy.

My mother had hidden the Star Charm on the island, at the St. Hestia Public Library.

At least we were pretty sure she had.

Miss Lettie, Mr. Sheppard, and I walked through St. Hestia's marketplace. It was like a bright carnival complete with acrobats and musicians and strange alien creatures wearing bright island shirts. Off the island, blending in with humans around the world, a lot of these aliens were like Mr. Sheppard: disguised in "human suits" walking the streets of Detroit or St. Louis; Paris, Texas and Paris, France; munching down deep-dish pizza in Chicago or teaching kids at South African schools. And every one of them was waiting—praying—for the time when they could go back to their *real* homes, free and unafraid.

The air around me was spicy with the aromas of barbequed chicken and fish. Cooks yelled over the crowds that their chicken or fish was the best and you should try it "before somebody else grabs up all this tasty goodness and go home!" Ice-cream vendors shouted out flavors I knew and flavors I didn't know. And women in floral print dresses sold fresh fruits and vegetables and fish and shell jewelry and hand-dyed clothes.

And everything was paid for in spells.

Miss Lettie bought me a new yellow blouse (five spells), a pair of really cute flower-print pedal-pushers (six spells) and a pair of New Balance sandals (regularly eight spells, on sale for six, plus she had a coupon, which brought the price down to five spells).

Some of the vendors we went to didn't want to take Miss Lettie's spells. Instead, they thanked her for curing their grandmamma. Or healing their little girl from night terrors. Or casting out a "skinwalker" spell—an evil spell wandering and whispering just beneath the surface of the skin—from their husband. One lady with a gold front tooth even thanked Miss Lettie for curing her cold.

"N'ua Ruba root tea done did de trick, sistah-woman!" the woman with the gold tooth laughed before showing the cold remedy power of N'ua Ruba root tea by inhaling deeply and exhaling through her snot- and booger-free nose.

Everywhere we went, people smiled and bowed to us. At first I thought they were smiling and bowing to Miss Lettie, since she seemed to be the GTG (Go-To-Girl) around here.

But they were all smiling at and bowing to me.

Some said "Your Highness," or waved to me like I knew them or something.

I smiled and waved back, not knowing what else to do.

After shopping, we walked along sandy roads and through fields of yellow and red flowers to Miss Lettie's house in a place called Solace Bay. Her house sat on the edge of a tropical rain forest near the beach. In the distance behind her house, and rising above the green rain forest, was a dark blue and cloud-white mountain called Tutu Biko.

Miss Lettie's house wasn't as nice a house as Miss Evelyn's, and you could kind of tell she lived alone. Hardly anybody else but her could fit inside her house.

The house was painted pink and green with a white front porch and all sorts of potted and hanging plants. Wind chimes were hung everywhere. On almost every side of her small house, gardens were bursting with flowers, herbs, and vegetables.

The porch faced the ocean, and maybe a hundred feet away, reaching out into the water, was a dock where little painted fishing boats bobbed up and down on the water. Old black men in red and orange and yellow and blue swim trunks and sleeveless T-shirts sailed the boats out on the water or sat on the rickety pier repairing nets, playing cards, or just talking and laughing.

"Are they Sky Conjurers, too?" I asked Miss Lettie as we sat on her porch.

"Oh, yes," Miss Lettie said. "Mostly retired. Dat one over dere, him from Nairobi. A healer. And dat one? Him worked in a car factory in a place called Lansing, Mitch-igan. Good men who conjured quiet, good spells for dey families, friends, and villages."

Miss Lettie had made us pineapple juice mixed with fresh lime and coconut milk. She had poured two big glasses with ice, and we sat quietly looking out at the fishermen.

After a while, Miss Lettie said, "I be sorry for all de trouble been caused you. Right to my soul, I be sorry."

I nodded, shrugged, and said, "S'okay, I guess."

"No," she said. "It's not okay. But on my honor—my life—I be makin' it right. For you and de spirit of your mother."

I asked her where Mr. Sheppard was. She said he'd gone into a different section of the marketplace to catch up with friends and to shop for "special things."

I didn't ask what the "special things" were.

After we finished our drinks, Miss Lettie said we needed to see the St. Hestia Public Library's head librarian. Since it was Sunday, Miss Lettie was sure the Head Librarian wasn't going to be happy with our visit. But for whatever reason, Miss Lettie said we couldn't wait for Aunt Monique to arrive.

Together, Miss Lettie and I walked along a narrow sandy path through berry bushes and high, green hills until we came to the home of the St. Hestia Public Library's head librarian.

"Highly irregular," the librarian said through the cracked round door of her house. By the way: Her house was only four feet tall and was made from dried seaweed, seashells, straw, grass, and stones. It looked like an island version of a doll's house. "Really quite unacceptable."

Miss Lettie was bent over at the waist, talking through the sliver of opened door.

"You know who dis be, don't you, Miss Peekaboo?" Miss Lettie asked, pointing to me.

"Well, of *course* I do," the little squeaky voice said with a bit of attitude. "I assure you I am neither blind nor stupid, Miss Lettie. It's the queen. And I really would like to throw 16,583 years of rules, regulations, and very detailed policies to the twelve winds, but it was the Sky Conjurer's Royal Court itself that set these rules for this library. And one rule clearly states no weekend visitors. The library needs the weekends to regenerate itself. To spread out. Stretch its limbs. Reorganize itself without anyone traipsing willy-nilly through the hallways, coughing, sneezing, whispering, or asking silly questions like where have the bathrooms disappeared to. Sorry, your Highness, but rules are rules—and who are we without rules? Have a nice day. Bye-bye."

The door slammed shut.

Miss Lettie knocked again.

The door opened a crack and the librarian heaved a big, tired sigh.

"One last question, Miss Peekaboo," Miss Lettie said. "How many Hunters with Dark Matter spells or Spirit Wands would it take to destroy de library? 'Cause however many you think dat might be, sister-woman, you may have double at your door any day. And when dey *do* come, de library's existence on dis planet will be gone in de blink of a Dark Matter eye. Poof!"

It was quiet for a few seconds. Then an even squeakier voice from inside the small house said, "Who is it, mommy?"

"Miss Lettie," Miss Peekaboo said. "Finish your frosted fish flakes and snog-worm roll-ups, dear one."

"Yes, ma'am," the squeaky voice said. "Hi, Miss Lettie!"

"Hello, Master Ofri," Miss Lettie said. "You be de good boy and listen to your momma, okay?"

"Yes, ma'am."

The door closed again and from inside I heard Miss Peekaboo say, "You have Ofri for the day, Joba. I'm going into work for a few hours."

"Of course, honey," another high-pitched voice said. "Don't be long."

The door of the small house opened wide and out walked what looked like an oversized gerbil in a floral print summer dress and big, round black-rimmed glasses perched on the end of her shiny eraser-pink nose. She walked on her hind legs and carried a really small black briefcase.

"I owe you for dis, sister-woman," Miss Lettie said with a respectful bow to the oversized gerbil.

"Oh, you *bet* you do, sister-woman," the gerbil said. "16,583 years of respected rules, out the window."

Miss Peekaboo stared up at me for several long, hard seconds, then cut her look back at Miss Lettie. "So this is Queen Yolanda's kid, eh?"

"Yes," Miss Lettie said. "Miss Charlemagne Althea Mack."

Miss Peekaboo looked back at me, sizing me up, which for a second was a hoot. After a couple seconds, though, I started to feel uneasy. Then Miss Peekaboo said, "For everybody's sake, I hope you got the stuff your mother did, kid."

Miss Peekaboo got on a silver scooter without wheels, punched a button, and a little engine whirled to life. The scooter rose into the air and Miss Peekaboo zipped off.

"See you there," she said before disappearing over a grassy hill.

After a ten-minute walk through fields of tall grass with the sound of ocean waves nearby, we reached the St. Hestia Public Library.

Back in the City, I'd always loved it when Uncle Joshua and Aunt Monique took me to the main library downtown; it was a huge old building with giant pillars and huge, shiny wood doors. Inside, it was cool and quiet and felt safe. I loved the way the marble floors felt and sounded when I walked across them and the way the high ceiling looked like a church. The library always excited me; it was a haven and there were thousands of books that wanted—begged for!—my attention.

But this library...

The St. Hestia Public Library had to be the biggest, most beautiful library I'd ever seen! It was a huge, blinding white marble and gold-metal building at least five city blocks long and reaching high into the tropical blue sky. There must have been thousands of stained glass windows wrapping around the building and spiraling up from floor to floor. At the top of the library was a giant gold-and-glass dome reflecting the sunlight, and around the dome were flags billowing in the ocean breeze.

"Dem be de flags of de twenty Sky Conjuring planets represented here on Earth. De homes people hope someday to return to," Miss Lettie said.

At the main entrance there were big, white marble pillars reaching up at least two hundred feet, and on either side of the tall stained-glass doors were two of the biggest, ugliest stone statues I'd ever seen. They looked like lions with wings and eagle talon feet. A small sign to the left of the big, glass-and-bronze doors of the entrance read, "Not responsible for lost articles, involuntary spirit possessions, or things that may stick to the bottom of your shoes."

The ugly lions squinted down at us, their gray stone eyes moving as we walked up the steps. I held on to Miss Lettie's hand.

Miss Lettie nodded to each of the lions.

"Afternoon, John," she said to one. To the other, she said, "Afternoon, Henry."

The ugly stone lions nodded their huge heads and said in voices that sounded like thunder, "Miss Lettie."

Inside, the library was cool and the only light coming in was through the big gold-and-glass dome hundreds of feet overhead. There was a fountain in the main lobby. Jets of ocean-blue water shot up and took different shapes—a book, a giraffe, my face—before splashing back into the pool. Floating above us was the biggest telescope I'd ever seen, pointing up at the sky through the dome.

"Thirty-eight million books, scrolls, Petra glyphs, hieroglyphs, crystal-glyphs, rune stones, griot drums," Miss Lettie said. "Three thousand rooms on most days—"

"'Most days'?" I said.

"Rooms come and go around here," she said as we walked to the long white marble checkout counter. "Sometimes, dey shows up. Sometimes, dey don't. A good library breathes like dat."

"Well," Miss Peekaboo's voice echoed, "come along, come along!"

Miss Peekaboo sat in a small chair on top of the white marble counter, facing a small computer. The normal-sized nameplate next to her read, "Miss Peekaboo Libris, Head Librarian."

She typed on her computer's keyboard with tiny, furry fingers, while staring through narrowed eyes at the tiny monitor.

"You seem to have a book overdue, Miss Lettie," she said. "*Molak Fig Gardening: Ten Spells for Juicier Figs.* Plan on returning this book anytime soon, or what?"

"Yes, Miss Peekaboo," Miss Lettie said with an impatient sigh. "Now, let's get on with—"

"You know, it's really quite unfair to anyone else who just might be interested in Molak Fig gardening," Miss Peekaboo said, adding a high-pitched "tsk, tsk." "Quite unfair indeed."

"Monday!" Miss Lettie shouted, her voice echoing off the high marble walls. "I promise!"

Miss Peekaboo peered over the top of her glasses at Miss Lettie, a little shaken up. Tell you the truth, girlfriend, I was a little shaken up. The sound of her angry voice was a big, fat smack of Keepin'-It-Real square in my face; we were here because a whole bunch of bad guys in black spacesuits wanted me way out of the way so they could get to the Star Charm. And they would do anything—and, girlfriend, I *do* mean anything!—to get me permanently gone.

"Of course," Miss Peekaboo finally said. "Now, then. What may I do for you, Miss Lettie?"

Miss Lettie nodded to me. I pulled the gold library card out of my pocket and handed it to Miss Peekaboo. Miss Peekaboo stared wide-eyed at the card before nervously taking it from me.

"Oh, my," she said turning the card over in her small, furry hands.

"What?" I said scared.

"This is a secured privilege card," she said. "We've only issued three of these in the past eighty years. One was to Queen Yolanda. One to her Ashanti Kai, code-named Joshua. And the other to—oh, my—"

"'Oh my' what?" I asked, feeling my heart stop.

"There was another card issued only twelve years ago," Miss Peekaboo said. "To a former member of the Ashanti Kai body. Someone code-named Morabeau. Alidus Morabeau—"

"Morabeau?" Miss Lettie said. "Why would Morabeau be issued a secured privilege card?"

"Before my time here," Miss Peekaboo said. "These cards allow passage to some of the more—how shall I say?—frighteningly awful, carnivorous, and dark-spell wings of the library."

"Carnivorous?" I said, a lump growing in my throat. "You mean like meat-eating? Y'all got rooms in this library that *eat meat*? Like *people meat*?"

"Well," Miss Peekaboo said sounding a little huffy. "Such—minor incidents—have been known to happen. When these rooms do appear at the library, my staff is very good about posting warnings and double-checking card access privileges. We've only lost three conjurers in the past hundred years. Frankly, I think that's an outstanding record."

I looked up at Miss Lettie and said, "Oh, girl, we are *so* out of here, it ain't even *about* bein' funny—"

Miss Lettie grabbed my blouse sleeve and held me at the desk.

"No, see, you don't understand!" I said to Miss Lettie, struggling against her. "I don't need to be no queen that bad! And I for-real don't need to be up in some freaked-out library that can chew my flesh-and-blood booty up like a ham sandwich!"

"Check de card," Miss Lettie said to Miss Peekaboo. "See when a dark-spell wing of de library last appeared and what was last checked out from it."

Miss Peekaboo pushed the card through a mechanical reader and squinted at her computer monitor. After a few seconds her eyes widened and her small furry mouth dropped open.

"Uh—twelve, ten, and five years ago, two dark-spell library wings appeared. Those are the most recent materializations. And it appears the last thing checked out was the Mesopotamian Enchantment Scrolls of Aga Moragusha Khan, 873 B.C.," she said. I saw her shudder. Then she said, "Very dark stuff. Very messy. But, uh—okay—here's the interesting thing. The scrolls are here. They're in the library, checked back in twelve years ago."

"What did Morabeau check out?" Miss Lettie said.

"Really, Miss Lettie," Miss Peekaboo said, peering over the rims of her round glasses. "You expect me to violate the reading privacy of the library's patrons? Certainly, you must appreciate—"

"What I appreciate," Miss Lettie said, holding her anger back as best she could, "is dat we may all be in de center of de Purifier's evil eye. Now, I must know what Morabeau checked out from de library, Miss Peekaboo—or I will be forced to use a spell to get dat information."

"Spells, rituals, and wand usage are strictly forbidden in the library," Miss Peekaboo said, her voice nervous and cracking. She and Miss Lettie gave each other mean looks for what felt like a long time.

Finally, Miss Peekaboo tapped a button on her keyboard and her computer screen went black. She crossed her small arms over her chest, stared at Miss Lettie through narrowed eyes, and said, "I'm going to the ladies' room to freshen up. I will know if you have tried to access my computer because whatever hand you use to touch my computer will be missing when I return." She paused, then said, "Of course, what with all the copper, bronze, magnesium, titanium, gold, and platinum fixtures in the ladies' room I may have a problem detecting whether or not you've broken sacred library rules by using a spell—a *quick* spell, mind you!—to discover what you need."

Miss Peekaboo hopped down from her chair and waddled off to the bathroom.

I looked at Miss Lettie and said, "So what's the worst that could happen if you use one little spell in here?"

Miss Lettie gave me a way-serious look and said, "I would be fined a thousand spells and lose my library visiting privileges for forty years. Plus John and Henry."

"Those ugly stone lions outside?" I said. "What about 'em?"

Miss Lettie swallowed hard, then said, "If I come within a hundred yards of de library before my banishment be up, dey will attack me. I trained dem, your Highness. Dey would surely get me."

"Okay, so like couldn't you just not tell Miss Peekaboo about the spell?" I said.

"A lie in silence be de same as a lie spoken," Miss Lettie said. "I won't dishonor myself or deceive Miss Peekaboo with such lies." Then she took a deep breath and said, "Stand back, your Highness."

A tornado of bright gold numbers and symbols began spinning around her. Some of the numbers and symbols flashed white before sinking beneath the caramel brown skin of Miss Lettie's forehead.

The tornado suddenly disappeared.

Miss Lettie opened her eyes and said, "Morabeau checked out almost every book in the Dark Earth Enchantment & Terribly Ugly Rituals section over de past eleven years. He asked de front desk several times for de location of the Mesopotamian Enchantment Scrolls of Aga Moragusha Khan. Nobody here ever find dem. When dat wing of the library appears, it usually be in section eleven, thirteenth floor, shelf—"

"Eleven, thirteen," I said, feeling my skin crawl. "November 13. That's—my birthday."

"Oh, my," Miss Peekaboo said returning from the ladies' room. She had actually put lipstick on under her furry snout and had rouged the fur of her cheeks. She turned her computer back on, adjusted her glasses, and squinted at the screen. "Section eleven, thirteenth floor. That particular section of the library seems to be in today and the scrolls are there, but it appears they're—uh— moving. At least three times since we've been here."

Miss Lettie looked down at me and said, "Stay here."

"What you say, girlfriend," I said feeling my body frozen right where I was standing.

Miss Lettie walked away from the desk, but Miss Peekaboo, still staring at her computer, said, "Wait a minute. Now they've disappeared."

Miss Lettie walked back to the desk.

"How could they—"

"No, wait," Miss Peekaboo said. "They're back."

Miss Lettie started to walk away again, but again Miss Peekaboo said the scrolls had disappeared from her screen. Miss Lettie walked back to the desk.

Miss Lettie looked at me and said, "I'm afraid you must come with me, your Highness."

"I don't want to do this," I said. My stomach was all bunched up and I felt like I was going to throw up. "I *can't* do this. Shouldn't Mr. Sheppard be here?"

"He'll be here if we need him," Miss Lettie said. "You must come with me, Miss Charlemagne. It appears de scrolls will continue to hide demselves if your presence is not felt."

"Didn't somebody say something about those scrolls being evil?" I said. "I can't deal with no evil scrolls, n'k? I'm twelve years old!"

Miss Lettie gently touched my forehead with her fingertips. Just like she'd done in the New Orleans graveyard before we went down into Mr. Sheppard's grave apartment. Once again, my body was floating.

"This is child endangerment!" I screamed. "You could get prison time for this, old woman!"

Miss Lettie looked at Miss Peekaboo, pointed a long, brown finger at the librarian and said, "Don't move."

"I—I think you can pretty much count on that," Miss Peekaboo said, nervously adjusting her big, round glasses on the furry bridge of her nose.

I floated behind Miss Lettie as we moved slowly across the lobby and up the wide main staircase.

"Uh—Miss Lettie?" Miss Peekaboo called out. "It appears the scrolls are preparing to disappear again."

Miss Lettie looked at me for a moment, then touched my forehead again. I felt my body become my own again.

"De scrolls must have sensed you were under a spell. Not moving of your own free will," Miss Lettie said. "De scrolls must know you are coming by your own choice, under your own power, your Highness."

"N'uh-uh," I said, a little dizzy from the spell. "Something up there doesn't like the fact that I'm breathing. I *like* breathing. It's a nice little habit my body picked up. Now, if you'll excuse me— I'm gone."

I turned to walk away.

"Den what did your mother die for?" Miss Lettie asked.

I stopped and turned to her, feeling the pain of what she'd said cut through me.

I walked back up the steps to Miss Lettie.

"I don't know," I said.

"And you never will," Miss Lettie said, "if you do not move beyond what frightens you into what enlightens you."

In the cool darkness leading up the steps I was too scared to say anything. On both sides were huge, gray stone statues of Sky Conjurers from other worlds. These were the first Sky Conjurers to come to earth. The ones who built the island of St. Hestia. The peach-fuzz hairs on the back of my neck stood up and I got creepy-crawly goose bumps; the statues' marble eyes were following us. One of the statues suddenly jumped in front of us, drew a giant stone sword and growled, "It's *Sunday*! We are not to be disturbed on *Sunday*!"

"Forgive us, Lord Malby of Talku," Miss Lettie said bowing her head. "But we must pass."

"I will allow your bodies to pass," the statue said with an evil laugh. Then he raised his stone sword and said, "But your heads will stay here to decorate my sword!"

The sword suddenly cut through the air.

Miss Lettie held up a hand and caught the blade of the sword as it was about to lop off our heads. The statue struggled against Miss Lettie's strength.

"Again," Miss Lettie said calmly, "we be humbled and honored by your presence, Lord Malby of Talku. Forgive our untimely intrusion."

Soon, the huge statue gave up his struggle and slowly put his sword back in its stone sheath. Grumbling in a deep and disappointed voice, the statue clump-clumped back onto his marble stand at the side of the stairway.

"Oh, yeah," I said to the statue as we passed by it, "that's what *I'm* talkin' 'bout, boy-oh. Mess with us one time!"

The statue sadly hung its head and grumbled, "Twice in one day. A *Sunday*! Doesn't anyone respect the rules anymore?"

Miss Lettie stopped.

"Twice?" she said. "Who else has passed this way, Lord Malby?"

The statue lifted its large stone head, nodded and said, "You and—"

The statue of Lord Malby began shaking violently.

Then he exploded. Chunks of stone that had been Lord Malby flew past us and thundered down the marble steps.

Miss Lettie shielded me with her body.

After a minute, the library was quiet again.

I looked up at Miss Lettie, shaking, and said, "I am definitely getting the feeling somebody doesn't want us here."

"Which means we exactly where we should be," she said.

We finally reached the eleventh floor. There were long, dark corridors lined with tall half-shadowed pillars. In the middle of the wide corridors were tables and chairs and lamps and high bookshelves. Very little light came in through the high, arched windows. "Okay," I whispered nervously, "so like, this is usually the part where some psycho brotha in a hockey mask jumps out and starts swinging an ax or chainsaw at the cheerleaders?"

"Are you a cheerleader?" Miss Lettie whispered back.

"Well, no, but—"

"Neither am I," she said walking ahead of me. "I guess we have nothing to worry about."

"No, see, like, my point is—"

She didn't wait to see what my point was. I didn't exactly feel like being left alone, so I caught up with her.

We rounded a corner.

I froze.

In the opened doorway of a huge room there was a man with a big, puffy Afro hairdo, on his knees in front of a burning electric guitar. Dancing around him was an older man in a big, white, floppy suit and slick black hair that was bouncing around. The older man had a big, wide, toothy grin and he was flinging a music conductor's baton from side to side.

"Music room," Miss Lettie said, barely looking at the two men. "I'll take you dere sometime."

"How 'bout now," I whispered.

"*You beeeetrayed meeee!*"

A man's angry voice hissed through the air.

"*You will pay in blooooood!*"

Shadows raced through the air above us.

We turned another dark corner.

Sitting at a long library table was the shadow of a man.

Miss Lettie fired up a couple of bright orange fireballs in the palms of her hands.

"Show yourself!" Miss Lettie shouted.

The man reached to the middle of the table and clicked on a lamp.

"Hello, Miss Lettie," the man said.

Seated at the table was a skinny man with pale white skin. He was dressed in a gray suit and looked more like an English teacher than some sort of conjurer of dark spells and evil magic.

"Morabeau," Miss Lettie said, hate filling her voice.

"The years have been quite kind to you," Morabeau said, smiling a crooked smile. "You look as bewitching as ever." He slowly raised his hands, laughed, and said, "I come in peace." Then he smiled at me and said, "Well, this must be our Miss Charlemagne Althea Mack. Some people say you are the new queen of the Sky Conjurers. Is this true, little girl?"

I didn't say anything.

"*You betraaaaayed me and you shall paaaaaaay!*"

Miss Lettie, Morabeau, and I looked up and saw shadows fluttering against the high library ceiling.

"Been hearing that since I got here," Morabeau said. "Really quite annoying after a while."

Something was behind Morabeau in the shadows, breathing hard. With a slow, echoing *click-click-click* on the marble floor, whatever it was got closer until it stopped at Morabeau's side.

"Say hello to the nice people, Trevor," Morabeau said, reaching out and gently petting the lowered head of a giant red scorpion with yellow sideways-blinking eyes.

I think I threw up a little in my mouth...

ENTRY ELEVEN:

Squaring Off

Okay, so I was too old for baby diapers.

And I was for sure way too young for adult diapers.

But, girl, all I know is looking at that giant scorpion I was about to drop all my messy business in my pants right then and there.

I was shaking, unable to take my eyes off the scorpion standing at Morabeau's side. And worse, the scorpion couldn't take its eyes off of me. With every stinking breath, strings of sickly yellow scorpion drool splattered on the library floor. The scorpion's huge, poison-filled stinger jittered above its head, waiting for a reason to stab anybody who wasn't Morabeau.

"You still be travelin' with de wrong kind of conjurers," Miss Lettie said, nodding to the scorpion.

"Don't you read the newspapers? Watch cable TV news? You simply can't have too much protection these days," Morabeau said. Have you ever wondered why you do the things you do sometimes?

Well, I was wondering why I was walking slowly toward Morabeau and his pet scorpion instead of running and screaming out of the library all the way back to the City.

"Stay behind me, girl-girl," Miss Lettie said. She tried to grab my sleeve, but I yanked my arm away and kept walking.

"Leave me alone," I said to Morabeau.

Morabeau smiled at me and said, "Dear child. Whatever makes you think I wish to do you any harm?"

I pointed to the scorpion, its eyes locked on me and its stinger raising.

I swallowed hard and said, "That—*thing*."

Morabeau turned and looked at the scorpion as if he hadn't realized a scorpion the size of a school bus was standing at his side.

"Trevor?" Morabeau said affectionately. "Oh, she's harmless really. Likes to play the role of protector. But at her heart's core, she's a gentle soul who enjoys long walks along the beach, playing Barbies, and listening to music—"

"Gee," a voice said from the top shelf of a bookcase. "Sounds like just the girl for me."

A shadow jumped down from the bookshelf and landed in the light between me and Morabeau.

Mr. Sheppard!

But this was a Mr. Sheppard I hadn't seen before. This was *DJ Smackdown* Mr. Sheppard! He was wearing a black jumpsuit and held a long, black stick up at the scorpion's head.

"If you don't want that stinger stuck where you sit, then you'll back off, Trevor."

"Well, well, well," Morabeau snarled. "If it isn't the formidable Mr. Sheppard. What's up, *dog*?"

"Long time, no see, Morabeau," Mr. Sheppard said, his eyes still locked on Trevor. "I see banks full of Earth money still haven't given you a bit of class, panache, style, or savvy. You're still the same old traitorous worm. Tell Trevor to back off, or I'll be barbecuing scorpion steaks on the grill tonight."

Trevor and Morabeau didn't move.

"Did I mention that this is an Altarian Series-7 Mythaloric Spell Accelerator?" Mr. Sheppard said. "I don't exactly know what it can do, since this is the only one on this planet. But I've heard they can be really ugly if you're on the wrong end of one."

Morabeau finally nodded to Trevor, and the giant red scorpion glowed blue for a few seconds before changing into a really pretty, really mean-looking lady with short, straight-black hair and a jammin' red leather three-piece suit with red patent leather high heels. Good look for a bad lady.

The lady in red stared angrily at Mr. Sheppard for a few seconds before returning her cold black eyes to me.

I walked closer to Morabeau.

Trevor tried to step in front of Morabeau, but Mr. Sheppard kept his spirit weapon under her chin.

"I would strongly advise you to stay back, your Highness," Mr. Sheppard urged.

I put my hand gently on Mr. Sheppard's shoulder and looked down at him. He glanced quickly up at me and I nodded.

"You sure, your Highness?" he said.

"I'm sure," I said.

Mr. Sheppard stepped aside but still kept his weapon pointed at Morabeau and Trevor.

"Leave me alone," I said to Morabeau. "I've never done anything to you. I don't even know you."

"You think *you* are what this is all about?" Morabeau asked, narrowing his eyes at me. "This has absolutely nothing at all to do with you, little girl. Your preteen troubles are nothing compared to the pain and suffering caused by a thousand years of war and slavery between Sky Conjurers and the Purifiers. Your concerns, my quaint little queen, are less than a speck of dust on the eyelash of a Gilgamesh Red River Dragon."

"I am Charlemagne Althea Mack," I said, taking one more step closer to him. "I'm an all-A Honors student at Jane Cooke Wright Middle School. I just thought you'd like to know a little about the person who's gonna jack you up if you mess with me or any of my peeps. See what I'm sayin', man?"

Morabeau stared at me blankly for a second. Then he smiled and said, "Okay, let's pretend for a moment I understood whatever it was you just said. How would you go about 'jacking' me up?"

I brought my hands up, and from the palms two large spinning balls of lightning shot toward Morabeau and Trevor. One ball of lightning hit Morabeau and lifted him out of his chair and high into the air. Trevor rocketed off the floor and slammed hard into a bookshelf.

Morabeau slowly picked himself up from the floor, his nice English teacher suit shredded and smoking. Trevor was knocked out.

"That's just a taste," I said, fighting as hard as I could against the fear that was spreading out across my chest. "Next time you get the whole cheese enchilada."

Morabeau looked down at his ruined suit and said, "Have you any idea how much this suit cost? Giorgio Armani, child? Ever hear of him?"

With a wave of his hands, a new suit draped itself over him.

He stared hard at Miss Lettie for a moment before saying, "You've trained her well."

"I've not trained her at all," Miss Lettie said. "Just tink what she be like when I do train her."

"Please believe me, ladies—and dog," Morabeau said, brushing invisible specks of dust from his new suit, "I have not come here to cause trouble of any sort. I've come to end troubles. The troubles we Sky Conjurers have continually endured for a thousand years."

"You've come for de Star Charm," Miss Lettie said.

"And what if I have?" Morabeau said, suddenly angry. "What if one piece of jewelry whose only power is unfulfilled promises and false hope could instantly send millions—billions!—of Sky Conjurers safely to their home worlds tomorrow! Rejoining their families, their friends, as free people. Who are you to deny them that chance for peace?" He stopped and took in a deep, ragged breath. "You would give that up just so we could live out our lives on this and other miserable planets? You're a fool, Miss Lettie! You made a fool out of Queen Yolanda, and you're making a fool out of her only child!"

"If de price of freedom be losing your own soul, it's not worth it," Miss Lettie said.

"Yo, hey," I said interrupting them. I looked at Morabeau and asked, "What do you get out of this deal?"

"Pardon us, little girl," Morabeau said, annoyed with me. "The grown-ups are trying to have a big-people conversation here. Why don't you wander off to the children's section of the library and find a book on poison apples or glass slippers or something?"

Mr. Sheppard fired a black bolt of energy from his spell accelerator at Morabeau's feet. A section of the marble floor exploded.

"The queen asked you a question, Morabeau," Mr. Sheppard said. "I suggest you answer it."

Morabeau glared at Mr. Sheppard for a moment before casually sitting down at the library table. He inspected his fingernails for a few seconds, sighed, and then smiled up at Miss Lettie, Mr. Sheppard, and me.

"For peace of such magnitude, it's only right that the one who negotiates it receive a reward, don't you think?" he said. "I mean, I wish I could be more charitable. But business is business wherever you go in this galaxy. My investment has been time and energy. And great personal risk, I might add."

"You risk de lives of others for your own personal gain," Miss Lettie said.

"Get to the point," Mr. Sheppard said, jabbing the energy weapon at Morabeau.

"You know, I never liked you," Morabeau said to Mr. Sheppard. "Personally, I always thought it was a mistake for the Sky Conjuring Council to approve you as Queen Yolanda's personal Starchaser pilot. I told them so. But they didn't listen. *She* didn't listen. Oh, and *now* look where Queen Yolanda is! Poof! Reduced to vapors, mist, and fond farewells!"

Mr. Sheppard nudged the end of his energy weapon under Morabeau's neck.

"Mr. Sheppard," Miss Lettie said quietly. "No. Dey be another time and place."

"I'm warning you," Mr. Sheppard growled at Morabeau.

"Warning *me*, you scruffy mutt?" Morabeau laughed even with the weapon nudged under his chin. He nodded toward me and said, "You should be warning *her* about what dangerous fools you and Miss Lettie are!"

Mr. Sheppard leaned into Morabeau and whispered, "Another time, Morabeau. You and me." Then Mr. Sheppard backed slowly away.

"If you'd both done your jobs properly," Morabeau said, rubbing the place beneath his chin where the weapon had been jabbed, "good Queen Yolanda might probably still be alive. But I suppose the truth is even royalty can't get good help these days."

"Listen up, Morabeau," I said. "You ain't dealin' with Miss Lettie. And you ain't dealin' with Mr. Sheppard. You dealin' with *me*. So, like, when I talk to you, you talk to me. I have seen my uncle die and I have been chased halfway across the funky-butt end of Louisiana. So the for-real truth is I am in no mood for you. You have stepped on my last good nerve. Now I asked you a question and since you old and probably don't hear so good no more, I'mo ask you again. What's in this peace deal for you if you give the Star Charm to these Purifier punks?"

Morabeau stared at me like he was itching to get this whole magic cage-match smackdown thing going.

Good.

I was sick and tired of being tired and scared.

"Child," he finally said, "I am trying to save people. And what I get out of this is of no importance."

"My name," I said, "is not 'child.' My name is Charlemagne Althea Mack—and I am a *queen*. Now, if you can't wrap your brain around that, then you and this Trevor chick can roll on up outta here and get seriously gone out of my life."

"Enough," a voice said from the shadows behind him.

My heart stopped and I suddenly felt very cold.

"I can handle this!" Morabeau shouted.

"You've handled nothing," the figure said, stepping into the faint light near Morabeau.

Aunt Monique...

ENTRY TWELVE:

And You Think YOUR Family's Dysfunctional?

I wanted to run up to her and hug her.

I wanted to feel her arms around me and know she would take care of me and make all of this nightmare go away.

Instead I stood frozen with fear and sadness as she stood next to Morabeau.

"If you'd simply let me—" Morabeau started to say to her.

Aunt Monique gave him a look and he shut up. Then she looked back at me and said, "Hello, Charley Mack. I'm sorry it has to be this way, baby-girl."

"Be—what way?" I said.

She walked toward me. Mr. Sheppard stepped in front of her, his weapon pointing up at her.

"I'm disappointed in you, Princess," he growled.

"Still," she said, looking at Mr. Sheppard like she was bored, "I am a Princess and you of all people should know the punishment for holding a weapon on a member of the royal family."

She waved a hand over the weapon and it flew out of his hands, disappearing over her shoulder into the darkness behind her. It clanged several times on the marble floor before it rolled to a stop.

"Miss Lettie," Aunt Monique said, "we mean no harm. We only wish to discuss the situation. Charley Mack, you asked what Morabeau got out of handing over the Star Charm to the Purifiers. Perhaps your question should be what do *I* get out of giving the Star Charm to the Purifiers." She looked at me and smiled a sad smile. "For years I've stood in the shadow of your mother, my sister. A Princess in title only. While she traveled from star system to star system on her Royal Starchaser and built her legend as a warrior and protector of the people, I lived an anonymous, powerless life. All for what? A war without end? Your mother should have negotiated with the Purifiers ages ago. She should have bargained with them instead of battling against them. She should have acted like a true queen instead of a dreamer on a fool's crusade. And she should have been more of a mother to you."

I was trembling, shaking uncontrollably. I felt cold and alone and frightened.

My heart was breaking.

I knew how I'd lost my Uncle Joshua.

I had no idea of why I was losing my aunt.

"You—you shouldn't talk about Mama that way," I said, feeling hot tears running down my cheeks. "She—she was a good person—"

"You know nothing about her!" Aunt Monique shouted. "She was nothing but a dream you could never touch!"

"Don't you say that. Please don't say that—"

"Whoever you think you are," Aunt Monique said, "you are still just a child, Charlemagne. And the future—the future of all Sky Conjuring People—cannot be decided by a child."

"Maybe she be exactly de one who should be making de decisions around here, Princess," Miss Lettie said from behind me. "As it's written in de *Book of Legends*, 'Every child is a message of hope sent into de future by those who may not live to see dat day.'"

"Words, old woman," Aunt Monique said. "Pretty words and nothing more."

"Mythaloricals," Miss Lettie said. "Dat's why you be here, too. Right, Princess? Queen Yolanda somehow left de same message in your mythaloricals as she did with Miss Charley Mack. Dat's why you said you'd meet us here tomorrow instead of today. By then, you would have found de Star Charm and none of dis would be happening." Miss Lettie sighed and shook her head. "Dem Bokubans back in de bayou. You called dem forth—"

"I did no such thing!"

"You brought dat tree down on your own leg," Miss Lettie said. "All so dat you could get to de scrolls before us." Miss Lettie lowered her head for a sad moment. I couldn't say anything. I stood watching my life being ripped apart by things I didn't understand. Miss Lettie raised her head. Her eyes were glowing. "But Queen Yolanda? She left de same message in you for another reason. She wanted you here, Princess. Not to claim de Star Charm. But for Miss Charlemagne to meet her true enemies."

I wiped the tears from my cheeks but they kept coming. It felt like I couldn't get enough air to breathe.

Aunt Monique stared hatefully at Miss Lettie, then looked back at me and said, "I do love you, Charley Mack. But this is bigger than any love that I could ever have for you."

"I—didn't think there *was* anything bigger than love," I said.

"The needs of the many must now outweigh the needs of the few," she said. "Or the one. When peace has been negotiated and the Star Charm is handed over to the Purifiers, then the Sky Conjuring People will need a true leader. A real queen. They will not need nor will they trust such a task to a twelve-year-old girl pretending to be a queen."

"So that's what you get out of all of this," Mr. Sheppard said to Morabeau. "Riches. Treasures from a thousand Sky Conjurer worlds in payment for peace. All with the Princess leading the way." Mr. Sheppard growled for a second, then said, "That isn't peace. That's trading one slave master for another."

Morabeau looked down at me with cold, gray eyes and said, "Riches are meaningless without power, Mr. Sheppard. Power is the true treasure. And a certain power leading the free Sky Conjuring People under the Princess is what I get."

"Get any closer to the queen, Morabeau," Mr. Sheppard said, "and you'll be wearing your scabby butt as an ugly hat."

Morabeau ignored Mr. Sheppard and said, "You appear to be wise beyond your young years, Charlemagne Althea Mack. Think about it. Doesn't your wisdom tell you that Princess Monique and I are doing the right thing? Search your heart."

I looked at him.

His thin, lying smile.

His cold gray eyes.

I thought about my Uncle Joshua. I could still see him lying on the cold, wet floor of the old apartment building's furnace room, buried under smoking rubble. He'd given up everything, including his life, for what he believed in. And mostly, he had believed in me.

"I've searched my heart," I said, looking at my aunt and at Morabeau. "Here's my answer."

I grabbed Morabeau's forearms and felt electricity crackling through my hands and into his body.

Aunt Monique quickly released a coil of white light toward Miss Lettie. Miss Lettie spread her arms to her sides and was instantly surrounded by a bubble of blue light. The coils of light from my aunt slammed into the blue bubble, bounced off, and exploded against the tall bookshelves. Books and papers flew into the air.

"Mr. Sheppard!" Miss Lettie yelled.

"I'm on it!" Mr. Sheppard yelled back.

Trevor was awake now and had changed back into the giant scorpion. She brought her sharp, poisonous tail down at Mr. Sheppard.

Mr. Sheppard jumped into the air, flipped, and landed on the back of the scorpion's stinger.

"You just don't get it, do you, Trevor?" he said, before pulling the stinger down to Trevor's neck.

Trevor changed back into the woman in the red leather suit. Two spinning kicks at Mr. Sheppard. He ducked both, jumped into the air, spun, and returned the favor. Trevor flew backward through the air, slamming into the burning bookshelf before crumpling to the floor unconscious.

Finally, Miss Lettie released a burst of energy from her right hand. The energy wrapped around Aunt Monique and trapped her inside.

"Release him, your Highness!"

It was Miss Lettie.

She was talking to me.

I didn't want to listen to her.

I wanted to fry Morabeau until the world was free of him.

Until I was free of him.

I kept the white electricity from my hands pouring into Morabeau's stiffened body.

Then I felt Miss Lettie's hand on my shoulder.

"Release him, Miss Charlemagne," she said softly. "You be no better dan him if you continue to hurt him."

I didn't want to let him go…

...but I did.

I released him and watched him slump into a heap to the library floor.

A shadow flew over us.

"*My brother!*" the shadow cried out. "*You betrayed me! You betrayed me—and you shall pay a thousand times in blood!*"

The Mesopotamian Enchantment Scrolls of Aga Moragusha Khan.

They were floating above me.

Cursing and screaming in pain, blood poured down from the scrolls and splattered on me.

Suddenly, the scrolls burst into flames.

The fire quickly burned itself out and black ash floated down through the air. In place of the scrolls there was a bright and shining necklace floating above me, its rainbow-colored jewels shimmering.

Everyone stared up at it.

It was the most beautiful thing I'd ever seen.

It came down and gently laid itself around my neck. I was scared, but I stood perfectly still as it clasped itself. I touched it. There was a sound. Like a small wind chime.

Then...

...golden beams of light spun out from the necklace and made a ring around me. Standing in the golden light were at least thirty women of all colors, sizes, ages, and shapes. Some were young. Some were old. Some were dressed in the green moss that grows on trees. Others were dressed in white, flowing silk and colorful bird feathers. And still others were dressed in white clouds or bronze armor or rags tied with rope at the waist.

And they were all bowing to me.

One of the women in the golden circle floated toward me. Her skin was the color of a ripe peach and her floating hair was golden like morning sunlight.

"We," the woman said in a voice that was both in the air and in my head, "are the living powers of the Star Charm. I am called Cerridwen, goddess of Death and Rebirth. And these," she said, sweeping a hand out to the other women, "are my sisters. Artemis. Brigid. Durga. Isis. Ix Chel. Yamaya. And many others. We are your servants and protectors. We guide the power you were born with and magnify it a thousand times. Our lives are in your hands, and yours in ours. Command us wisely."

"Did you—know my mother?" I asked.

Cerridwen bowed again and said, "Her spirit is within each of us now, true and strong. Perhaps some day she will be born among us as a goddess in her own right."

"Can I—talk to her?" I said.

Cerridwen smiled and said, "You can always talk to your mother. And she will always hear you. But when she speaks, you must use your heart to listen."

"Uh—okay, so like, I'm pretty new at this," I said. "Just how do I get in touch with you guys? Just in case, you know, somebody tries to boost my crib or mess me up or something?"

"Miss Lettie will show you the way."

And with that, she floated to Mr. Sheppard and Miss Lettie.

She smiled at them and said, "You both seek forgiveness for things that do not require forgiveness. You served Queen Yolanda well. And now, without past regrets or yesterday's sorrows, you must do the same for this one."

Miss Lettie began crying.

Mr. Sheppard nodded that he understood.

The goddess named Cerridwen floated back to me and said, "We feel your great power and potential, your Highness. But there is still much to be done. If you doubt your abilities—if you doubt your heart can meet the coming challenges—you must tell us now and we shall leave and await the one who will come after you.

Know this, though; if we must wait for the one after you, millions of people on hundreds of worlds will die as slaves. Choose."

I looked back at Miss Lettie and Mr. Sheppard.

They were looking at me.

Then I looked at all the women standing in a golden circle around me.

They were looking at me.

"Okay, so, like here's the deal, girlfriend," I said to this Cerridwen chick. "I'll take the job on one condition."

"There can be no conditions—"

"Yeah, well today there are, girl," I said. "I need me some kickin' threads. Like y'all got. Except you," I said pointing to the goddess dressed in a rag bag roped at the waist. "I don't even know what that is."

Cerridwen smiled at me and nodded.

"You shall have clothing that befits your status," she said. "Listen well to Miss Lettie. Know that Vorkasku Ronin Ran is your friend and protector. And above all, trust with your whole heart in the person you are. Without such trust in yourself we, the goddesses of the Star Charm, are of no use."

Cerridwen floated back to the circle of women.

They all bowed and said, "May you live long, Queen Charlemagne. May you reign wisely. And may we serve each other well."

Then...

...on separate beams of golden light, the women disappeared back into the Star Charm around my neck.

I looked at Mr. Sheppard and said, "Vorkasku Ronin Ran? That's your real name?"

"It means 'Mountain Rising to Meet Morning' in Altarian," he said. "You can still call me Mr. Sheppard."

I looked at Miss Lettie and said, "Does this mean it's over?"

"Every goodbye ain't gone," Miss Lettie said. "Every shut-eye ain't asleep."

"What she's trying to say in her homey little way is this is far from over, little girl," Morabeau said, struggling to his feet.

The blue bubble imprisoning Aunt Monique disappeared and she fell to her knees, gasping for air.

"You have no idea what you've done," she gasped. "You've brought the Hunters and Purifiers down on all of us with your stupid little game, Charlemagne."

"I think my mother would've—"

"Your mother is *dead*, Charlemagne!" Aunt Monique shouted.

"There is nothing more to be done here," Miss Lettie said, standing in front of me and looking down at my aunt. "Princess, please. You must—"

"*You* must *shut up*, old woman!" Aunt Monique said, jumping to her feet and pushing Miss Lettie aside. She shot out her hand to me and said, "Give it to me, Charlemagne! Give me the necklace!"

Suddenly, something exploded against the ceiling and for a second spread orange fire and black smoke.

Everyone froze.

A small, squeaky voice said, "Library hours are Monday through Friday, 9 A.M. to 8 P.M."

Miss Peekaboo.

She was struggling to hold on to Mr. Sheppard's Altarian Series-7 Mythaloric Spell Accelerator weapon.

"Now, if you please," she said, walking toward us, the energy staff wobbling dangerously in her tiny hands, "I would greatly appreciate it if you all left the library—my library—right now. I am seeing a mess. I am not happy about seeing a mess in my library."

"This is not over, old woman," Aunt Monique said, pointing to Miss Lettie.

"I didn't tink it was," Miss Lettie said.

Then Aunt Monique looked at me.

"Don't be a foolish little girl," she said. "Leave with me now and I promise you will rule as you truly should."

She held her hand out to me.

I looked at her hand for what felt like a very long time.

It was the hand that I'd held as a little girl crossing streets in the City. It was the hand that had held me, made me feel secure and safe. From her hand I'd felt love and happiness and warmth on the coldest days of the longest winters.

Finally, I looked up at her.

I held out my hand to her.

"You can still roll with my crew," I said, nodding to Miss Lettie and Mr. Sheppard.

"I'm sorry," Aunt Monique said, lowering her hand. "I cannot do that."

She turned and walked away.

ENTRY THIRTEEN:

Secrets & Truth

Mr. Sheppard, Miss Lettie, and I offered to help Miss Peekaboo clean up the mess, but I think she'd had enough of us for one day.

"It'll be a miracle if I don't report each and every one of you to the Council," Miss Peekaboo said, looking around at the mess. She looked like she was going to cry. "This is no way to treat a library."

Miss Lettie, Mr. Sheppard, and I walked back to Miss Lettie's house. On the long walk back through tall grass and bright flowers, none of us said anything. Mr. Sheppard walked ahead of us, occasionally stopping to sniff the air before continuing his four-legged trot with his Spell Accelerator wand strapped across his back. Miss Lettie and I walked in silence, only inches apart.

Even though the sun was bright and the sky was the bluest I'd ever thought a sky could be, it still felt like a dark and awful day to me.

Here I was wearing the most beautiful and powerful necklace on the planet. A necklace only the Queen of Sky Conjurers could wear. And it felt like I'd lost everything that I ever cared about just to wear it.

My mother had worn the Star Charm, and she was gone.

My uncle had fought to protect me and the Star Charm, and he was gone.

And now my Aunt Monique had sacrificed the memory of my mother and my uncle and was ready to give me up for this stupid hunk of metal and stone hung around my neck.

Ain't no gems or jewels worth losing family over.

Miss Lettie fixed a lunch of fresh fruit, vegetables, spicy dried fish, and a pitcher of ice-cold papaya juice lemonade. I didn't eat or drink any of it. All I wanted to do was find the darkest corner of the planet, ball up in it, and cry myself into a long, dreamless sleep.

"You got to eat, girl-girl," Miss Lettie said. "Got to keep your strength up."

"I'm not hungry."

I just sat on the porch staring out at the dark-skinned old fishermen, throwing their nets out, hollering to each other, shooing away seagulls, bobbing around on the waves in their colorful little boats like bathtub toys on shiny blue water.

Mr. Sheppard trotted back and forth near the edge of the beach, looking out over the water and up at the sky.

Guard duty.

After a while, Miss Lettie sat next to me on the porch. She didn't say anything for a long time. Then she said, "We must begin your *Capoeira Bimba Conjurus...*"

"No more," I said. "I'm not doing anything else until somebody downloads the 4-1-1 on what's going on. Why did Morabeau say you and Mr. Sheppard caused my mother's death?"

"Your Highness—"

"No!" I said standing. "Enough is enough, Miss Lettie! I'm not doing anything else until you tell me the truth! All of it!"

Miss Lettie looked down at her folded hands, then nodded her head. "I will tell you," she said. "All of it."

And she did.

Miss Lettie had once been one of the most highly respected and most powerful conjuring arts teachers in the Sky Conjurer Royal

Court. As a teacher, she was never to get personally involved in the lives of her students. She was never to care about them beyond their education.

She was never to feel love.

She began teaching my mother when my mother was six years old. It didn't take Miss Lettie long to realize my mother was special. Gifted as a conjurer and leader beyond what Miss Lettie had ever seen.

In my mother, Miss Lettie saw a goddess. She saw the prophecies of something called *The Book of Legends* coming true.

"'A goddess will come,'" Miss Lettie said, quoting from the book, "'with a wisdom beyond her young years and a spirit that reaches beyond knowing. This One will teach the teacher. This One will bear the fruit of a New Future.'"

Miss Lettie believed with all her heart that *The Book of Legends* was talking about my mother.

"You would not have wanted to know me then, Miss Charlemagne," Miss Lettie said. "I was cold. Unfeeling. I saw only young, undisciplined minds. Not hearts. Not spirits. Your mother, she changed me."

Miss Lettie broke her vow of staying out of my mother's life beyond enchantment teachings.

She broke her vow of not loving.

The Council of Sky Conjuring Governesses discovered her change of heart and told her she could no longer be my mother's teacher.

"If Miss Lettie's sin is to love, then all of your greatest virtues are of less worth than her sin," my mother told the Council. "And if her punishment is to be banished by the Council, then I offer you my thanks—for now she is free to become my personal Royal Truth-Teller."

A "truth teller" is somebody a queen or king counts on to tell them the truth no matter how bad the truth may be.

When my mother was fifteen, she became the queen. Two years later, the wars between the Sky Conjuring People and the Purifiers spread like fire across the galaxy.

The Royal Sky Conjuring Council wanted to move the royal family far away to a distant and safe world. A place where they could live in big, fancy palaces under pretty pink skies. A place far away from the wars.

My mother thought this was a seriously stupid idea.

"She tell de Council, 'What good is a queen if she does not fight for de cause of her people? What good is a monarchy if it only serves itself?' She took up de cause of her people," Miss Lettie said. "She stood shoulder-to-shoulder with conjurers and warriors from a hundred worlds to defend their right to live as free people."

Miss Lettie fought at my mother's side.

Mr. Sheppard helped them escape from a planet where slave Sky Conjurers rose up against the Purifiers but lost the battle.

"Mr. Sheppard, him a scientist," Miss Lettie said. "Highly respected Altarian scientist. Designed and built the first Starchaser spaceships. Fastest ships in de whole Sky Conjurer fleet. He wasn't no pilot, though. And he wasn't no fighter. But in him your mother saw greatness. A true friend. She believed in him. Sometimes having somebody believe in you is all it takes to become great."

My mother, Miss Lettie, and Mr. Sheppard traveled a long time before finding the place the Sky Conjurer prophets of *The Book of Legends* had talked about. A magical island hidden on a blue planet in a far uncharted corner of the galaxy.

My mother risked her life bringing escaped slaves to Earth.

"On one trip, she told me and Mr. Sheppard to stay here. To prepare St. Hestia for the Sky Conjurers who had escaped de Purifiers," Miss Lettie said. "She said we couldn't go back with her into de Purifier territories. It be too dangerous and dat she did not want to risk our lives. Mr. Sheppard and me, we argued with her—

but she was de queen. And sometimes being loyal to someone you love means doing things you tink maybe shouldn't be done. Instead of Mr. Sheppard and me, she took two Ashanti Kai—the one you know as Joshua, and the one now known as Alidus Morabeau. Dey were to be da protectors of da One and the Many."

After several journeys into dangerous Purifier space, my mother thought it was best if Uncle Joshua and Morabeau stayed behind to organize the refugees on St. Hestia and to set up the Sentinel stations around the world. Piloting a passenger shuttle herself, my mother set out to bring even more thousands of escaping slave Sky Conjurers to Earth.

"Of course, Mr. Sheppard and me, we followed her," Miss Lettie said. "To make sure she was safe. But—we were followed."

It was when my mother began her last trip to Earth that a remote Hunter scout ship spotted her ship.

On the dark edges of the Frontier they fought.

My mother's ship was destroyed and everybody on board was killed.

"Mr. Sheppard and me destroyed de Hunter scout ship. We towed de wreckage as far away from dis star system as possible. We let the pieces of dat ship float around a distant and barren world. Something to throw the Purifiers off. Mr. Sheppard and me, we come back here to find out why de queen had sacrificed her life. Her sacrifice was for you, Miss Charlemagne. Her only child. She wanted you to be born in freedom."

Miss Lettie looked at me, her eyes flooded with tears.

"I—I be so sorry, Miss Charlemagne," she said.

All I could do was stare at her.

After a while, I stood up.

I looked down at Miss Lettie and said, "You let her die."

Then, I slapped her hard across her face and ran inside the house.

ENTRY FOURTEEN:

Royal Court Press

I sat at Miss Lettie's small, round kitchen table for a really long time. Staring at nothing. All of my sadness and fear and confusion made my body feel heavy.

Out of the corner of my eye, I saw Mr. Sheppard walk up on the porch and sit next to Miss Lettie.

"You told her, didn't you?" he whispered.

Miss Lettie nodded her head.

Mr. Sheppard put a paw on her back and said, "It's for the best. I apologize to you, Miss Lettie, for not having your courage."

Again, she nodded.

They sat quietly for a few minutes, Mr. Sheppard's paw gently patting her back. Then he said, "Shall I have a talk with her?"

Miss Lettie shook her head no.

The sun sank into the ocean and night took over. None of us had moved from where we sat in silence. Each of us getting beat up by our own awful thoughts.

One of the old dark-skinned fishermen walked up to the house. He handed Miss Lettie a note and she opened it. After reading it, she looked at the old fisherman and said, "Thank you, brother-man."

The old fisherman nodded and walked away.

Miss Lettie got up from her seat on the porch and came into the house.

"De Council wish to speak with you tonight, Miss Charlemagne," Miss Lettie said.

I looked up at her.

I didn't say anything.

"Miss Charlemagne," she said. "I have caused you much hurt and for dis I am truly sorry. After you speak to da Council tonight, I promise you will never have to see me again."

Miss Lettie bowed and walked to one of the back bedrooms of the small house. She closed the door.

Mr. Sheppard trotted inside and stood in front of me.

"I'm as much to blame as Miss Lettie," he said. "Perhaps even more. You are free to give up on me, your Highness. But please don't give up on Miss Lettie. Whatever her failures have been, they are minor compared to the triumphs of her conviction and her love."

Mr. Sheppard bowed and walked out of the house, back to guard duty on the beach.

The stars were jazzing up the dark night sky. Miss Lettie came out of the back bedroom. She was dressed in a white floor-length silk caftan with a gold silk shawl draped across her shoulders. Around her neck was a necklace made from small white seashells and tiny yellow flowers.

"It be time," she said.

I stood, and we walked out of the house.

After what felt like forever, we came to the side of Tutu Biko Mountain and walked into a cave. On the walls of the cave, torches lit our way until we stood in a large, bright chamber. The high walls were white marble and blue glass. On each side of the chamber entrance were stone tablets with weird writing on them.

Miss Lettie kissed her fingertips, then touched one of the stone tablets.

"De *Book of Legends*," she said.

Mr. Sheppard gave his right paw a lick, then touched the same stone tablet.

Sitting at a long, curving, blue glass table under floating balls of yellow and white light were three men and four women. All of them wore white robes and gold shawls pretty much like Miss Lettie.

The woman sitting in the middle of the Council table stood and tapped a huge wind chime hanging from the high ceiling of the cave.

"In honor of all we have loved," the woman said, "and to all who will set the feast table for us in the next life. In honor of the children who will carry our message of hope into the future, I declare this session of the Sky Conjurer Earth Exile Council in session." The woman looked at me, smiled, and said, "I am Lona, your Highness. Since you are new here among the people, just think of me as the mayor of St. Hestia. These," she said, gesturing to the other people sitting at the glass table, "are my Councilors. We have requested your presence to speak on a very grave matter: Your troubled ascension as our new queen and the coming of the Purifiers."

Miss Lettie bowed low to the Council and said, "Permission to speak, Lona."

"You don't need to ask for permission, Miss Lettie," Lona said, taking her seat at the Council table.

"I must ask dat I be excused from dese proceedings," Miss Lettie said. "I ask dat you give our queen a new governess. One who might serve her better."

Mr. Sheppard stood and said, "I too must ask that the Council assign a new protector to the queen. One more capable than myself."

"If this is what you wish," Lona said. "I'm not quite sure I understand why…"

"It's because of me, Miss Lona," I said, raising my hand. "Uh— like, can I say something or should I just, you know, shut up?"

"Of course you may speak," Lona said, smiling at me. "You are the queen. You may say whatever you wish, whenever you wish."

"Cool," I said nervously.

Being twelve years old and surrounded by adults in white silk robes was kind of a new thing to me. They all looked at me like they were actually going to listen to me.

"Okay, so like, here's the real deal," I said, taking a couple steps toward the Council table. "I'm probably not as good a speaker as my mother was, but here goes: Miss Lettie and Mr. Sheppard want to quit because they think I blame them for my mother's death. In a way, I guess I do. Truth is I've been looking for somebody to blame for a long time. Mostly, I've blamed myself. Truth is, Miss Lettie and Mr. Sheppard have become like family to me. And that scares me. Family always seems to leave me. My mother. Whoever my father was. My uncle and aunt. I guess I was just trying to push Miss Lettie and Mr. Sheppard away—'cause—'cause I just don't want to lose them, too."

I looked at Miss Lettie and Mr. Sheppard and said, "Seems like a whole bunch of bad magical *ju-ju* is goin' down, y'all. And most of it has my name on it. Truth is, I don't think I'm gonna get outta this alive without you guys. I need you, Miss Lettie. And I need you too, Mr. Sheppard."

I stopped talking

The Council chamber was silent.

After awhile, Lona said, "The queen has requested you remain at her side, Miss Lettie. You also, Mr. Sheppard."

Miss Lettie looked at me and smiled.

Then she bowed to me and to the Council and said, "I will serve as de queen wishes."

Mr. Sheppard looked at me and I winked at him.

He bowed and said to the Council, "I too will serve as the queen wishes."

"If there is no further discussion on this matter," Lona said, "we will move on. Your Highness, three days ago a Hunter attacked you, Princess Monique, and the Ashanti Kai code-named Joshua in the human city. Two days ago three Bokubans attacked you at one of our most important Sentinel Outposts. We have concluded that the Hunter and his Bokubans were a long-range scouting team sent deep into these undiscovered star territories. We have also concluded that the Hunter will continue his search for you and all other Sky Conjurers in this star system and on this planet. It would no doubt take days—weeks at the most—before other Hunters and their Purifier masters discover our place on Earth. Once we are discovered, they will not only endanger the lives of every Sky Conjurer in exile here, but also the humans born of this Earth. We request a discussion on what course of action to take to safeguard our people. We will begin this discussion with our other guests."

Lona gestured behind me, Miss Lettie, and Mr. Sheppard.

My aunt!

Standing with her were Morabeau and Trevor.

"No!" I shouted.

I held out my hands, hoping bright balls of electrical fire would spin out at them.

Nothing happened.

"Spells don't work here," Miss Lettie whispered to me. "Dis be a sacred place. Only ideas and faith work here."

"How can you let them in here?" I shouted at Lona. "They're the ones trying to hurt me!"

"They are Sky Conjurers, too, your Highness," Lona said calmly. "We are one family with different voices—"

"Yeah, well, they are *definitely* from the side of the family nobody likes," I said.

I looked back at Aunt Monique, Morabeau, and Trevor. They all bowed to the Council.

"Punks," I said.

"Honored members of Council," Aunt Monique said, walking toward the Council. She walked right past me without even *looking* at me! "We are here because as you so accurately stated, Hunters and Purifiers will most certainly find us on this planet. The threat is real. Not only will we be at risk, but the people born of this planet—the humans—will be at risk. Their lives. Their oceans and rivers. Their enchanted natural resources. We can end this threat without harm to anyone. We must give the Purifiers the Star Charm in exchange for peace. The Star Charm is what they fight for. With it, they will no longer need the millions of Sky Conjurers they keep as slaves. As a former Ashanti Kai, Alidus Morabeau knows much of the ways of the Purifiers. He knows they will accept this offer. And he knows they will honor it. The Star Charm has always been a symbol of power and of peace. If peace can be attained by giving it to the Purifiers, then I say it has completed its mission and fulfilled the prophecies of the *Book of Legends*. I pray you and the members of Council will see this urgent situation as we do. Thank you."

Aunt Monique bowed and walked past me again without looking at me. I felt my heart sink.

Lona nodded to me and said, "Your Highness?"

I looked at Miss Lettie and whispered, "You should probably do the talking. I'm not very good at talking in front of people, especially grown-ups."

"I, your Highness, am not de queen," Miss Lettie whispered back. Then she smiled and said, "You been doin' real good so far, Miss Charlemagne."

I nodded to Miss Lettie, then cleared my throat.

"Okay, so like, see it's like this," I said, hearing how truly ghetto stupid I sounded. "Uh—did y'all know Trevor here can turn herself into a scorpion? I mean, that can't be good, right?"

Dumb and dumber…

I cleared my throat again and said, "Okay. I'm not real good at getting up in front of people and talking about really important stuff. But I do know a lot of people had a lot of faith in my mother. And the right thing for my mother was fighting against slavery. I'm starting to understand that the Star Charm is more than just a piece of jewelry. It's the history of millions of people. So like, what's the use in being free if all of your history's been taken away? I guess what I'm saying is, if y'all wanna give up the Star Charm to these Purifiers dudes, I'm cool with that. But that doesn't mean I'll give up fighting for what my mother fought for. I don't know if y'all know about a human named Martin Luther King Jr. He was a great human who believed in freedom for all people. He was murdered. But the idea of freedom for all people didn't die with him. It's not gonna die with my mother. And it's not gonna die with me. Y'all want the Star Charm? Fine. Diamonds and rubies ain't nothin' but stones, and gold ain't nothin' but metal. But my mother's dream? I dare anybody here, standing or sitting, to try takin' that away from me. I guess that's about all I got to say. Y'all be cool. Right on."

Behind me Morabeau whispered to Aunt Monique, "This was your *absurd* idea to come here!"

"Quiet, fool," my aunt whispered back.

"Now that we have heard from the queen, others are welcomed to present their thoughts and feelings," Lona said. She pointed to the back of the Council chamber.

The Sentinel!

Mr. Trinidad!

He bowed to the Council and said, "Just flew in from Louisiana, and boy are my arms tired!"

I laughed.

Nobody else did.

"Honored members of Council, esteemed guests," Mr. Trinidad said, bowing. "As you know I am the Sentinel for Outpost 12,

Precinct 3, in the Great State of Louisiana. If you will allow me, I'd like to tell you a little story."

I liked Mr. Trinidad's stories, so I was looking forward to this one.

Mr. Trinidad's story went like this: Whenever it rained hard, a bird called a turkey buzzard just sat on a fence and scrunched himself up. The longer he sat the wetter he got. He'd cry to himself and complain about the rain. He'd say, "I'm gonna build myself a house! That way I'll never get wet again when it rains!" But when the rain was over, all he did was stretch out his wings, shake off the water, and warm himself in the sun. "What's the use building a house?" the turkey buzzard said. "The sun's out! Ain't no use being indoors now!"

"We," Mr. Trinidad said, "cannot afford to be like that old turkey buzzard. When the Purifiers come, what house will we take our refuge in?"

He turned and pointed to me.

"*She* is our house," he said. "Just when I was starting to wonder what in the name of gas planets I was doing in Louisiana, Miss Charlemagne Althea Mack reminded me why I was there. Why I was important. Why every Sky Conjurer's life is important.

"Even as exiles from our home worlds, we all took a vow that whatever planet we escaped to, we would try in quiet ways to be of service to those who were born on that planet. I am one of twelve Sentinels stationed around this planet that you have entrusted us to watch the skies for the safety of our people. You have also asked that we observe the humans of this world in hopes that we might quietly learn from them and possibly share our knowledge, our spirits, and our magic with them. This is what we've learned about our exile home: as I speak in this very time and space on this planet Earth, there are more than *27 million human slaves here—many of them children*! They are ruled throughout the day by violence and held captive by fear at night.

"As conjurers from other worlds collected in exile on this Earth, we know what it means to be slaves. But how are we to keep a vow of helping others if we are too scared to help ourselves? And if we can't believe in the magic of our children, what's left that's worth believing in? I ask the Council to look again into Miss Charlemagne's eyes. Only then will you see what I see. A magnificent queen. She is the true Orisha. Thank you for your time. And don't forget to visit Louisiana for the best Delta blues and Cajun music, crawdaddies, and catfish around! *E'toi, mon ami!*"

"Thank you, Sentinel," Lona said, smiling.

Mr. Trinidad walked to me and said, "How'd I do? I didn't sound stupid or anything, did I?"

"You were great!" I said. "But if you're here, who's watching the outpost?"

"I am," he said with a wide grin. "See, I'm not really here. What you see isn't really me. It's a three-dimensional holographic biocast image. Kind of like a copy of me made from light and with atomic density and dimension. The point is I'm still at the outpost. Just think of this as a long-distance call."

He began fading.

"Well, your Highness," he said, waving. "Gotta go. I'll keep an eye out for you!"

His right eye began flashing green before he disappeared.

Lona stood and said, "If there is no more to be said, the Council will adjourn to consider all points that have been made this evening. We will gather again in two days to offer our decision. Your Highness?"

"Yes, ma'am?"

"What we decide does not mean you are obligated to obey," she said. "But please understand we have the best interest of all Sky Conjurers here and on other worlds at heart."

"Yes, ma'am."

Lona tapped the huge wind chime, and the members of the Council stood and bowed to me.

"Now, your Highness," Lona said, "the Council must discuss the situation further and pray for guidance in reaching a decision."

Lona bowed to me, then led the Council members out of the chamber.

I turned to leave just in time to see Morabeau lean into my aunt's ear and growl, "We tried it your way, my dear Princess. Now we do things my way."

Morabeau shot an ugly look at me, and then he and Trevor stormed out of the chamber.

Aunt Monique was staring at me.

It wasn't a threatening look.

It was a look I'd seen in her eyes when I was five years old and had nearly walked in front of a bus. It was a look that said she was suddenly really, really scared for me.

ENTRY FIFTEEN:

The Deadly Art

"Thank you, your Highness," Miss Lettie said as we walked out of the cave.

"Ain't about a thang, girlfriend," I said.

Then I took her hand and held it.

Standing at the entrance to the cave were hundreds—maybe even thousands—of people. They were all staring at us, holding torches and lamps and small white balls of light.

A little girl with pale white skin and straight black hair made her way through the crowd and stood looking up at me. In her hands were two marble-sized balls of pink and green light. She carefully put the marbles of light at my feet.

"I made them myself, your Highness," she said.

I knelt down, picked up the balls of light, and held them in the palm of my hand. They tickled.

"Oh, yeah?" I said. "Well, let's see what these rascals can do."

I threw them as high into the air as I could. They exploded like July Fourth fireworks against the night sky. (Okay, so I added a little something extra to them.)

The crowd cheered and started calling my name: "Char-le-magne! Char-le-magne!"

For a few seconds I imagined these same people had once shouted my mother's name the same way.

This was the beginning of a party that lasted all night long and way on into the morning. Musicians played and acrobats whirled through the air, and there were dancers in strange, colorful costumes, and elephants decorated with gold headdresses, and giraffes wearing long necklaces of seashells and silver beads.

And food!

"All this is for me?" I asked Miss Lettie.

"It is for you," she said.

Later that morning was a little different story.

I don't know how long I slept, but I can tell you it wasn't long enough.

Miss Lettie whispered in my ear, "Time to wake up, your Highness."

I rolled away from her, grumbled something mean, and tried to go back to sleep.

"Time to rise," she said. "We must begin your training. We must begin de *Capoeira Bimba Conjurus.*"

"Y'all go on ahead and start without me, n'k?" I grumbled.

The woman just wouldn't go away!

She pestered and prodded and shook me until I was very awake and not at all happy about it.

Miss Lettie had laid out new clothes for me: a pair of black chimney-legged pants, a long black sleeveless T-shirt, and a white silk rope belt. Not exactly my style, but cool enough.

I stumbled into the clothes and shuffled out to the front porch, yawning and stretching all the way. The morning air was chilly and the sun was just beginning to inch above the horizon.

Miss Lettie was standing on the beach with someone.

A man.

They were both dressed in red pants with gold silk rope belts and long red sleeveless T-shirts.

I shuffled half asleep down to the beach, not at all happy that I wasn't catching at least four more hours of Zs.

When I finally got to where Miss Lettie and the man stood I was ready to give her a piece of my suddenly royal mind.

But, *giiiiirl*, the brotha standing next to her...

Definite hottie!

I mean for an old guy in his, like, thirties.

He was tall with dark brown skin, perfect white teeth, big, puppy-dog brown eyes, muscles that had muscles, and a smile that could make molasses run like water.

"Yo," I said to the man. "S'up?"

The man bowed to me and said, "Your Highness."

Wait a minute.

Hold up.

I *knew* that voice.

"Mr. Sheppard?" I said.

"Yes, your Highness," he said. "Like my new human suit?"

"Uh—yeah," I said, embarrassed. "S'cool I guess."

"Vastly improved version," he said. Then he held up his hands, flexed his thumbs quickly and said, "Thumbs work perfectly!"

"Uh—yeah," I said. "Them thumbs definitely got it goin' on."

"We must begin," Miss Lettie said. "Princess Monique and Morabeau will not stop until dey possess de Star Charm. Dey will not wait for de Council's decision. You must prepare for battle, your Highness. You must learn de ways of de *Capoeira Bimba Conjurus*."

"Uh—the wha?" I asked.

"De *Capoeira Bimba Conjurus*," Miss Lettie repeated. "Or as it is sometimes called—de Art with a capital A. It be one way a warrior fights."

Miss Lettie said it was a very old style of self-defense. Sky Conjurers had learned it a long time ago from African slaves who had been shipped to Brazil to work in the sugarcane fields. It was a combination of dance, gymnastics, and martial arts. It was how the slaves defended themselves once they escaped from their Portuguese slave masters.

"Mr. Sheppard and I will give you a demonstration," Miss Lettie said.

I looked at the new, improved Beef-Cake Mr. Sheppard and said, "You *go,* boy."

In a flash, Miss Lettie and Mr. Sheppard twisted and leaped and flew past each other. They somersaulted and cartwheeled and did handstands with their legs spinning in the air like helicopter blades. There were low, sweeping kicks and high jabbing punches.

A couple of times when they were both high in the air they threw fireballs at each other. They ducked and dodged the fireballs that exploded into the sand or plunged into the ocean, foaming and steaming.

This was way more than a demonstration, girl.

It was an off-the-hook, witch-and-wizard smackdown.

"Stop!" I yelled, afraid they were going to hurt each other. "I think I get the idea."

They both bowed to me. Miss Lettie walked up to me and said, "Tell me one of your fondest memories of de one you call Uncle Joshua."

It wasn't hard to remember: Our bus rides to and from the City League Gymnastics Club. How he taught me to concentrate. To focus my mind and body. To reach down deep inside and bring out better than the best in myself.

I looked up at Miss Lettie.

She smiled and said, "Now, do you understand?"

I nodded that I did.

She looked at Mr. Sheppard and said, "Two hours, Mr. Sheppard. History, philosophy, and movement of de Art. I be teachin' her defense spells dis afternoon." Then she took a deep breath and said, "To become a master of de Art can take a lifetime. You, my queen, have only today." Then she looked up at the sky and quietly said, "It be comin', yes-yes."

"What's coming?" I asked, suddenly wide awake and scared.

"Your greatest challenge," she said.

Miss Lettie brought her eyes down from the sky. Her eyes suddenly became wide as she looked at me. She stumbled back a step.

"Mr. Sheppard!" she called out. "Come quickly!"

"What?" I said. "What's going on?"

I reached up to touch the Star Charm around my neck.

Then I looked down: the charm and necklace were slowly sinking under my skin.

I screamed.

"Not even your mother—" Miss Lettie whispered.

Scared, I began picking at the necklace, trying to rip it from around my neck.

Miss Lettie grabbed my hands and held them away from my neck.

Watching the Star Charm sink beneath my skin, she nodded and said, "You are de *One*."

"What's going on?" I asked, crying. "What's this thing doing to me?"

"It is becoming part of you," she said. "And you are becoming part of it. De Star Charm has accepted you far more dan any other queen who has worn it. Your powers be far greater dan any of us expected, your Highness."

The necklace was now completely under my skin. In its place was a golden tattoo that was an outline of the Star Charm necklace.

Miss Lettie let go of my wrists and I carefully, gently touched the golden tattoo on my chest and around my neck.

"Okay," I said after taking a deeply frightened breath, "so, like, am I gonna have to wear, like, tunics and turtlenecks the rest of my life?"

"De *Book of Legends* foretell of de Star Charm becoming a living being when De One is found," Miss Lettie said. "You, Miss Charlemagne, be De One."

Okay, so can we talk about *pressure*?

Miss Lettie and Mr. Sheppard bowed to me.

After a few seconds, they stood up from their bow and Miss Lettie said, "Now, you must practice, your Highness. Your great powers will mean no-ting if you do not know how to focus and use dem wisely."

She nodded to Mr. Sheppard. Mr. Sheppard said, "I'd like to apologize in advance for this, your Highness."

Then he grabbed my arm and flipped me high into the air.

I flapped around like a stupid rag doll in the air and landed hard on my butt in the sand.

"Hey!" I said. "Didn't you hear Miss Lettie? I'm *The One*, brotha-man! You ain't supposed to be treatin' *The One* like this!"

Apparently, Mr. Sheppard didn't hear me.

For the next two hours I left butt prints all up and down the beach. The old fishermen in their colorful boats pointed to us, laughing and whistling and cheering. Sometimes they let out loud groans when I splatted face-down on the sand.

One of the fishermen hollered, "Kick dat old dog's furry *be-hind*, your Highness!"

I tried.

Oh, girlfriend, I really, truly tried.

It was starting to look like seven years of gymnastics training and knowing how to survive the streets of the 'hood weren't nearly enough to keep sand from being pounded into my butt.

Mr. Sheppard wasn't holding anything back: spinning legs and somersaults, backward and forward flip kicks, crouching leg sweeps and windmill arms. It was all there. And it all had me right in the middle of being thrown, flipped, whipped, and twisted.

Finally, I'd had enough.

With sand in my mouth, hair, eyes, ears, belly button, and butt, I just sat on the beach sweating and trying to catch my breath.

"Isn't the Star Charm supposed to help me?" I said.

"Only your spirit will help you," Mr. Sheppard said, standing over me. "Your spirit is the energy that ignites your powers and the powers of the Star Charm. You must demand more of your spirit. Where you once would give up is now where you must begin. Fear is the enemy. Virtue is the key. Determination and focus are the fire."

I lifted my head—which felt like twenty pounds of hurt in a ten-pound bag—and looked up at Mr. Sheppard.

"Come on, Mr. Sheppard. I'm just a kid," I said. Then I dropped my head and tried to catch my breath.

Mr. Sheppard sighed, then said, "Perhaps I was wrong about you. Perhaps you *are* just like your mother."

My head snapped up and I glared at Mr. Sheppard.

"Yes," he said squinting down at me. "Just like your mother. Weak and lazy and undisciplined. All talk."

"You'd better *step off*, Mr. Sheppard," I shouted.

"Yes, just like her; done before you even begin," he continued. "A weak mind, feeble spirit, and lazy body."

"Cut it *out*!"

"Why should I, child!" Mr. Sheppard yelled, thumping his huge human-suit chest with his big human-suit fists. "Because *talking* about your mother hurts? Because you want to curl up and cry like a wet-diaper baby? You are weak! Just like your mother!"

I was on my feet, fists balled up tight.

Three forward flips.

Handstand.

Spinning legs.

My feet connected with Mr. Sheppard's chest.

He went sailing through the air, landing hard in the sand.

I suddenly had two crackling balls of lightning spinning in the palms of my hands.

"Your Highness!"

I saw his face.

Wide-eyed.

Afraid.

Slowly, the balls of lightning faded back into the palms of my hands and, crying, I said, "Why?"

"Because every Sky Conjurer on this planet and worlds beyond is depending on you," he said. "Because *I* am depending on you. And we only have one shot at making all that is wrong, right."

"What you said was awful," I said. "Mean and ugly and cruel."

"What I said," Mr. Sheppard said, "is where Morabeau will begin. If you cannot control your anger—if you cannot focus and push yourself beyond exhaustion and hurt and fear—then you will not win. And millions of people who know you as their queen will lose."

I slowly nodded that I understood.

"Your heart is where your true strength is, your Highness," he said. "That is where real magic lies. Trust your heart."

We practiced for another hour.

This time, the old men in the fishing boats didn't say anything. Instead they studied us. Nodded their heads in approval. I could feel what they were feeling. They had been on Earth long enough to hope I was The One. The Orisha.

Funny thing about hope, girlfriend.

It's easy to put your hopes in someone or something else. But when people actually put their hopes in *you*, it makes you feel small and clumsy. Like maybe they mistook you for somebody else. Somebody taller, stronger, smarter, and braver.

That's how I was mostly feeling.

After an hour more of *Capoeira Bimba Conjurus*, I was dripping with sweat.

As we walked up to Miss Lettie's house, Mr. Sheppard said, "You *are* just like your mother."

I looked up into the smiling face of Mr. Sheppard's human suit.

"Strong," he said. "The heart of a lioness."

"Or a goat," I said.

We walked into the house.

Miss Lettie was standing, staring at the kitchen table. She looked like she'd just seen a ghost.

At the center of the kitchen table was a black flower vase full of flowers. The flowers had thick, long green stems and colorful blossoms that looked like the beaks of tropical birds.

I reached out to touch one of the flowers. Miss Lettie grabbed my wrist and held my hand back.

"Don't," she said.

The flowers began screeching, their long, colorful blossoms snapping like hungry mouths with needle-sharp teeth.

"Yakti flowers," Miss Lettie said. "Dey feed on de flesh and bones of small animals."

Miss Lettie handed me the note that had come with the creepy flowers. It was from Morabeau.

"The little one and I settle this tomorrow," the note read. "At the Breathing Time."

⟙

ENTRY SIXTEEN:

The Ceremony of Spirits

"I can't do this."

Miss Lettie had fixed a dinner of fish, vegetables, fruits, and spiced breads. Women and kids from all over the island brought cakes, cookies, chocolates, and flowers that didn't have teeth. The men brought small, handwritten notes—blessings—and tucked them into the floorboards of the front porch and around the door.

All the food and flowers and notes felt like visitation hours at a funeral home. And the dead person everyone had come to see laid out was me.

"I can't do this," I said again, sitting at the kitchen table and staring off into space.

People weren't supposed to be depending on me for anything. Nobody should be depending on a twelve-year-old black girl who'd lost a gymnastics competition and got kicked out of school and didn't have any family any more.

"Your Highness," Mr. Sheppard said, using a paw to nudge a plate of fruit my way, "you need to eat. You must keep your strength up."

I looked down at him.

He had changed out of his human suit and was back to his scruffy, brown-spotted dog self.

"I can't do this, Mr. Sheppard," I said. "This isn't my life. This is somebody else's life."

"I would be lying if I said I know how you feel," he said. "No one can truly know how you must feel right now. But the one thing you must believe is that you are stronger than you think you are. And you are braver than you ever thought possible."

"Good doesn't always win over Evil, ya know," I said. "I mean I know that, n'k? I lived in a city where Evil kicked Good's butt all the way around the block every day and night and twice on Sunday."

"Then don't try," Miss Lettie said. "You be free to give up, Miss Charlemagne. Dat's your choice."

"I didn't ask for this! I didn't ask for *any* of this!"

"No one asks for de life dey be given," Miss Lettie said. "You just do what you can with de life you have."

"And look at me!" I said, not listening to her. "How am I supposed to give Morabeau the Star Charm anyway?"

The Star Charm was all the way under the skin around my neck. The only thing left was a golden tattoo of it.

Miss Lettie narrowed her eyes and stared at me for a moment. Then she said, "Only one way to release de Star Charm from you."

"Okay!" I said. "*Now* we're talkin'!"

"You must give in to all of your fears," she said. "You must be willing to give up hope."

I stared at her for a second. Then I said, "Well, there you go, girl! I can do that!"

There was a knock on the screen door.

I must have jumped about a foot up out my chair.

It was the little girl who had given me the two marble-sized balls of light at the party the night before.

She was holding a single red rose.

"I brought this for you, your Highness," she said.

Then she laid it in front of the door and started to walk away.

I looked at Miss Lettie, then at Mr. Sheppard, then to the girl as she made her way down the porch steps.

"Wait a minute," I said to the little girl. "Hold up."

I went out to the porch, picked up the rose, and said, "I didn't catch your name last night."

"Moya Akora," she said. "Most people just call me Mo."

I sat down on the porch steps and she sat next to me. She looked up at me and gave a great big grin. She was maybe seven or eight. But with Sky Conjurers, who can tell? She could have been a college senior for all I knew.

"Well, Moya Akora," I said. "Why'd you come here?"

"To see you," she said. "Before The Breathing Time."

"You know about that? You know what's happening?"

She nodded and said, "Everybody does."

"Call me Charley Mack," I said giving her little shoulder a nudge with my arm. "I—I guess I'm a little scared is all, Mo."

"That's pretty normal for older people like you," she said. "But besides my mom and dad, you're the bravest person I know, and that's honest."

I put my arm around her shoulders and we sat quietly for a couple minutes just looking out at the last bits of sunset over the ocean.

"How'd you like to be my bestest girlfriend in the whole wide world, Mo?" I said.

She jumped to her feet and said, "Really? Honest?"

"Honest," I said.

"So, like—what do I have to do? Is there, like, a ceremony or something? A ritual?"

"Yeah, actually there is," I said. "A very special one."

She lowered her voice, brought her small face close to mine and whispered, "What is it?"

"Tomorrow afternoon, you and me have to go into the village and try to eat all the ice cream on this island."

"That's it?" she said sounding a little disappointed. "I thought there'd be, like, a blood oath or something. Maybe we'd spit on each other's hands and shake."

"That's a nasty boy thing," I said. "Trust me. Eating ice cream is a lot more fun and much cleaner."

"Okay," she said with a shrug. "Sure."

"It's getting late, Mo," I said. "You should go home and get a good night's sleep. Dream about you and me and all the ice cream you can eat, n'k?"

"Okay," she said smiling. Then she started to walk away. She stopped, turned back to me, and said, "Can I tell my friends we're bestest girlfriends?"

"Sure," I said.

She grinned wide and walked away.

I turned and looked at Mr. Sheppard.

"Make sure my bestest girlfriend gets home safe."

Mr. Sheppard nodded and began trotting behind Mo.

I went inside the house.

Miss Lettie was standing and smiling at me.

"Moya and her family come from a planet called Echelon," she said. "Been here for ten Earth years. Echelon was once a very enchanted, peaceful planet. Mostly farmers. Fishermen. Da Purifiers come and enslaved those who couldn't escape. Made de slaves work in mines digging out stones of enchantment. Now, dey's only a thousand—maybe two thousand—Echelonians spread throughout the galaxy. Living in exile. Living in fear. Hoping someday soon dey can go home, free to grow crops and share meals with family and friends again."

I said, "Did you just say all that so I'd change my mind about calling this whole thing off?"

Miss Lettie nodded.

"Too late," I said. "Mo already did that. So what do we do now?"

"We pray," Miss Lettie said. Then she looked over my shoulder and said, "Welcome, my brothers and sisters."

I turned. Twelve people stood at the door. Most of the men I recognized; the old black fishermen that I'd gotten used to seeing out in their boats, bobbing around on the water. Some of the women I'd seen in the village, selling spicy chicken and fresh vegetables and fruits, hanging tie-dyed dresses on lines for the sun to dry.

They were all dressed in purple robes with high collars and trimmed with gold braid.

With the men on one side of me and the women on the other and Miss Lettie behind me, we all walked down to the beach.

The men and women made a circle around me. One of the women touched soft-smelling oil to my forehead, neck, and bare feet. Then she walked back to her place in the circle. One by one, the men and women walked up to me, each placing one end of a rolled-up piece of white silk ribbon in my hand and whispering in my left ear: "*Peace.*"

The circle of men and women walked once around me and I felt the ribbons of silk gently bind my hands to my chest.

One of the old men said, "We are the circle of your ancestors who have dreamed of your birth. You are at the center of our prayers and we are the foundation where you will build the future. In you are our hopes. In us is your strength. And in the heavens our triumph shall be." Then the men and women all kissed the end of their piece of silk ribbon. After the kiss, they circled back until the ribbons were loose in my hands again.

They raised their arms and hands over me until it looked like a canopy over my head. Closing their eyes they sang a song:

We are here for you,
You are here for us
Under this sky
To our rebirth amongst the stars
Family of the past
Children of the future
Only our spirits shall last
Only our spirits shall last
Forever, our spirits as one shall last

After they sang, one of the women handed me a white candle and lit it. The twelve men and women walked up to me, lit their own white candles from mine, bowed to me, and said *"Peace."* In a line, they walked away until they disappeared along the dark shore.

Still holding the candle, I turned to Miss Lettie and asked, "Now what do I do?"

"Now," she said, "you eat. Den you rest."

As Miss Lettie and I walked back to the house, all I could think about was what I was going to wear to this witches and wizards beat-down. Weird, huh? I mean this could be my last breathing night on Earth and all I could think about was what I was going to wear. I mean, you simply *don't* wear floral pedal-pushers, white tank top, and Nikes. Too touristy. And my black *Capoeira Bimba Conjurus* suit lacked a certain edgy flair. That little bit of something a girl needs to say, "Yo, hey! Bet you wish you looked *this* good, girlfriend!"

When we got back to the house, Miss Lettie gave me a big white box with a big red ribbon and said, "Open it."

I did.

Inside was simply the most off-the-hook, way-cool outfit I'd ever seen!

There was a black sleeveless waistcoat with a padded banded collar that swept around the neck and swooped down to a short front zipper ending just above the belly button. The jacket also had slant-cut pockets and on the left pocket were my initials—"CAM"—embroidered in gold thread.

The slacks were a pedal-pusher style, only the legs had a way-cool flare off to the sides.

The whole ensemble looked and felt like leather. But knowing how Miss Lettie felt about animals, I really doubted it was leather. Then again, I didn't think it was that stupid fake *pleather* stuff.

"Oh, this is *da bomb!*" I said, looking at Miss Lettie. "Thank you!"

I hugged her.

Then I looked for the other box.

You know.

The shoes.

"No shoes, no boots," Miss Lettie said. "You have Jupiter feet, your Highness."

"Okay," I said, feeling a little hurt. "Are you saying, like, my feet are too big?"

"No," she laughed. "Jupiter feet are powerful feet. Much conjuring energy in dem. Much spiritual vitality."

Great, I thought.

Here I was with the coolest outfit I'd ever seen in my whole entire life and I was going out there barefoot. Looking like some Super Cotton-Picking Girl.

I ate a little—the butterflies fluttering around in my stomach really didn't let me eat much.

Then Miss Lettie tucked me into bed.

She sat at the foot of my bed for a long time before I said, "You can if you want to."

"Can what, your Highness?" she said.

"Kiss me goodnight."

My eyelids drifted shut and as they did I felt Miss Lettie's warm lips touch my forehead.

"Goodnight, your Highness," she whispered.

I wish I could tell you I slept like a newborn baby in her momma's arms.

I didn't.

I dreamed about dragon's teeth and scorpion stingers.

Don't Start Nothin' Won't Be Nothin'

"It's time."

Miss Lettie's voice drifted into my ear.

I woke up, looked at her, and nodded.

Sitting on the edge of my bed I tried to think about everything that had happened and everything that was going to happen. The longer I sat on the edge of the bed, the more it felt like I was on some sort of wild roller-coaster ride; moving too fast to think, and picking up speed.

I dressed in my new outfit.

Look good, stay sharp, be cool, I thought.

I took a deep breath, exhaled slowly, and walked out to the kitchen. Miss Lettie and Mr. Sheppard were waiting for me.

"We can take you only as far as Solanis Ridge," Miss Lettie said. "After dat, we—I—"

I walked to her and took her hands in mine.

"This isn't gonna be my mother all over again, Miss Lettie," I said. "There's a new sheriff in town, n'k? And her name is Charlemagne Althea Mack."

She smiled nervously and nodded.

Mr. Sheppard slapped me five with his paw and said, "Follow your heart—"

"And lead with a solid right punch," I said, nudging his furry chin with my fist.

Then I walked to the screen door, turned to them, and said, "Let's get this party started."

It was dark and cold and the sky was bursting with stars. I'd seen the sky like this one other time—on the island of Martha's Vineyard with Miss Evelyn. The Breathing Time. What looked like a barely visible golden haze on the surface of the black ocean was really the earth exhaling a long and magical breath.

We walked for a long time through the sleeping villages, the empty marketplace, past the looming shadow of the St. Hestia Public Library, along a dark path on the outskirts of the rain forest, and finally to the crooked road leading up to Solanis Ridge.

Miss Lettie and Mr. Sheppard stopped. I turned to them.

"Well," I said. "This is it, huh?"

They both nodded.

"May de goddesses be with you, your Highness," Miss Lettie said, bowing to me.

Mr. Sheppard took several steps toward me and said, "The rules of a Breathing Time confrontation say that Morabeau should be alone. Of course, considering it's Morabeau we're talking about, he may very well have Trevor at his side. Keep the cliff side of the ridge always in front of you, never at your back."

I nodded, then turned to walk away.

Then I ran back to them.

I hugged Miss Lettie and said, "I love you."

I felt her arms wrap around me and she kissed me on top of my head. "I love you, too, Miss Charlemagne."

Then I knelt and hugged Mr. Sheppard.

"I love you," I said to him.

"My heart is forever yours, your Highness," he said before licking my nose.

I stood and walked into the darkness that led up to Solanis Ridge.

Off to the sides of the narrow dirt path in the darkness I heard hissing and the snapping of small, sharp teeth. Yakti flowers, hungry for the blood and meat of a small animal.

After what felt like a very scary and very lonely forever, I reached the top of the ridge.

It was grassy and almost flat. At the far edge, Solanis Ridge dropped straight down for a couple hundred feet to the dark, churning ocean water below. There were tall, jagged rocks pushing up out of the ocean, and even in the darkness I could see waves crashing against the rocks and white spray flying into the air.

"Fade and evade," I kept saying to myself. "Float like a butterfly, sting like a—"

Shiny gold particles began zipping through the air.

The Breathing Time had started.

"Well, hello again, your tiny-ness."

Morabeau.

I turned quickly and there he was, standing a couple hundred feet away from me. I had my back to the cliff.

Oops.

Standing next to him was Trevor in a black leather pantsuit with knee-high black patent leather boots. This girl was seriously "America's Next Top Evil Model."

"S'up, peanut-head?" I said, feeling my heart banging hard against my chest. "Yo, hey, man—that's not even fair," I said, pointing to Trevor. "It's just supposed to be you and me. The rules say—"

"Rules, as they say, were made to be broken," Morabeau said. "Especially when they don't quite fit my needs."

"Yeah, but, see like—"

"Let's skip the eloquent middle-school chitchat, shall we?" he said, casually walking toward me. "You have the Star Charm. I want it. I'm a big, bad, scary adult. And you're an itsy-bitsy widdle girl. Before we explore any other clichés, what say we just conduct a simple transaction and we can all just go home, okay?"

"The Sky Conjuring Council hasn't made their decision," I said.

"Oh, well, you know how things go when grown-ups get involved," Morabeau laughed. "Talk, talk, talk and nothing gets done. Me? I'm a man of action. For example, when I first came to this planet, I tried the whole nameless, faceless, living quietly-and-poorly thing. Didn't quite suit me. So why not use one's natural abilities to get ahead in life? I've made oodles of money, dated some really dumb really beautiful movie actresses, and eaten in the finest restaurants around the world. All because I took action, dear! And I would suggest *you* take action right now by removing the Star Charm from your scrawny little neck before something really scary happens to you."

I took a few steps closer to him, stopped, and said, "Are you just plain monkey-dumb? Is that what your problem is?"

"Charming to the last," Morabeau laughed. His laughter stopped abruptly and he shouted, "Give me the Star Charm! Now!"

My heart raced and my brain felt like it was going to explode, but I started walking toward him, making sure to put a little more home-girl flav-ah in my step.

"Even if I did give it to you," I said, "you weren't about to negotiate with the Purifiers, were you? I bet you were gonna keep the Star Charm for yourself."

"Oh, my!" Morabeau said with fake surprise. "A flicker of intelligence from *mon petit Princess*!" He quickly dropped his act and growled, "Of *course* I was going to keep it, you little wretch! Once I have the Star Charm—and you *will* give it to me!—*I* will be the power the Purifiers will have to negotiate with! The Sky Conjurers haven't taken any action to save their own skins for a thousand years! Why should I bother saving their skin for them!"

"My aunt sacrificed everything because she thought you'd help bring peace," I said. I wanted to shoot fireballs and lightning bolts at him. I didn't. *Cool head*, I thought, *fade and evade*.

"Oh," Morabeau said as if he'd forgotten something, "and speaking of your beloved aunt…"

Out of the darkness a large blue bubble appeared. Inside was Aunt Monique. She was screaming, banging her fists against the sides of the bubble. The bubble stopped between Trevor and Morabeau. He smiled a crooked smile up at my aunt.

"You know, I really shouldn't make these things so airtight," he said. "But, that's the kind of guy I am. Did you know Sky Conjurers, especially royal born and bred Sky Conjurers, can lower their heart rate long enough to survive in the vacuum of space for up to three hours? But they have to remain calm. Your aunt doesn't look calm, does she?"

"Let her go," I said.

"Give me the Star Charm," he said, "and we are done here. You can skip all the way home and play Candyland with the Princess."

I looked at my aunt.

Her eyes were pleading with me. I didn't know if she was faking it, but my heart said no way.

I looked back at Morabeau.

"You just broke the biggest rule of all, Morabeau," I said.

"Gee, really?" he said with a cruel smile. "And what might that be?"

"Don't start nothin', won't be nothin'."

Morabeau scowled at me before turning his back to me.

"Trevor," he said jabbing a thumb my way. "I grow tired."

Trevor nodded.

Trevor's eyes turned sickly yellow as she changed herself into the giant scorpion I'd seen at the library.

Only this time she was a lot bigger, way uglier, and with much more of a drooling problem.

She gave an ear-shattering screech and ran toward me.

I looked down at my Star Charm tattoo.

It wasn't doing anything.

No glow, no shimmer, no bright lights, no goddesses.

I looked up.

Trevor was almost on me. Her claws snapped and her poisonous tail flexed, ready to strike.

Instead of running away, I ran toward her.

Jumping into the air, I flipped twice and landed on her back. One of her claws reached around and slammed hard against my side, knocking me off her back. I landed with a thud on the dew-covered grass.

Clapping.

Laughter.

"Stellar performance!" Morabeau cackled. "Really brilliant! And me without my video camera!"

Trevor was standing over me, growling. Gross and nasty-smelling yellow saliva dripped from her scissor mouth. Her tail coiled back, the stinger ready to strike. I rolled to the right. The stinger sliced through the air and hammered itself into the ground. Jumping to my feet, I crouched and ran under the scorpion's hard shell body.

"You rollin' with the wrong friends, Trevor," I said, standing behind her.

Wiggling her stinger free from the ground, Trevor spun around and shook the black sky with a horrible screech.

Three quick forward flips away from her, then two white balls of lightning at the ground directly in front of her. The lightning exploded, throwing dirt into her eyes. She screamed.

Trevor jabbed blindly at me with her stinger.

And where were my so-called goddess-girlfriends? Not a one of them was in sight! What's the use of being Queen of *anything* if the people who are supposed to work for you don't show up?

With a single-arm handstand, whirling my legs like airplane propellers, I hit Trevor's stinger hard and tore it away from her scorpion body. Gallons of sickly yellow poison splashed out from her broken stinger, burning the ground it fell on.

I ran.

Trust me, girlfriend—my two legs were no match for her six.

She caught up to me and we circled each other.

She jabbed her snapping claws at me. They grabbed for me like giant scissors. Trevor kept coming, her sharp claws snapping and her mouth hungry for the main course of *moi*.

"Finish her!" Morabeau yelled.

I had no choice.

I began running to the edge of the cliff.

Trevor took the bait and ran after me.

The closer I got to the edge, the more I started thinking this was a really bad idea. Maybe even the worst idea in the whole history of ideas.

A few short feet from the cliff's edge I dropped to my knees, sliding on the damp grass, stopping only inches from flying over the edge and smashing on the jagged rocks below.

Trevor couldn't stop.

She was too heavy and had built up too much speed.

She tried to slow her huge scorpion body but couldn't. Trevor went over the cliff's edge, tumbling end-over-end down. I fired two fireballs at her, each one exploding hard against the shell of her huge scorpion body, pushing her harder and faster toward the jagged rocks below.

Hitting the rocks, the scorpion exploded into green and brown slime that coated the rocks for a second before the ocean waves washed the rocks clean.

I turned to Morabeau.

"I drink my milk," I yelled to him. "I eat my vegetables and I take my vitamins. I don't cuss, smoke, spit, or eat pork. Now you got to ask yourself: How absolutely *bad* do I want the Star Charm? You got an answer, or you just wastin' my Pretty Girl Time?"

"Enough!" Morabeau shouted.

He ran for me and I ran to meet him.

Our legs whipped hard and fast against each other, arms and fists flailing at each other. Jagged bolts of lightning lit up the dark sky.

"I usually don't fight little girls," Morabeau said, preparing to come at me again. "However, you're a so-called queen, so I'll make an exception just this once."

"I thought you were gonna bring it," I said. "I thought you had *game*. Man, you fight like a *boy*."

More kicks and spins. I made hard contact with a leg-whip and brought Morabeau down to one knee. Dizzy, he shook his head, then looked up at me with a split and bleeding lip.

"Did I fail to mention who it was that let a Hunter Scout ship know where your dear mother was?" he snarled, standing and walking in a wide circle around me.

I felt my heart stop.

"Three guesses," he said, touching his split lip. "*Correct-o-mundo*! Me!"

He caught me off guard with two hard kicks that sent me tumbling backward.

"Your mother could have ended this a long time ago," he said, standing over me. "I tried to reason with her, but she treated me like a go-fetch dog. She was a fool!"

"She was a hero!" I screamed, feeling my ribs throb with pain.

He laughed. Then in a harsh, hurtful voice he said, "She was an ugly, useless joke just like you, you wretched little beast!"

I was angry and fighting back tears.

"Don't say that," I said. "Don't you dare talk about my mother like that."

"'Don't you dare talk about my mother like that,'" he said in a whiny little-girl voice, making fun of me. "The Great Sky Conjuring People in all their glorious wisdom have sent a weepy-eyed, rope-haired child to challenge *me*! A silly little girl with silly little ideas about what a picture-perfect fairy-tale world it would be if only she were a Princess or Queen!" He bent down and brought his face close to mine. "Well, you knotty-haired little troll—go back to whatever crumbling slum rock you crawled from beneath and stay out of the big people's way. Give the Star Charm to me now and I'll free your suffocating aunt."

I looked up at the bubble where my aunt was trapped. She was slumped against the side.

I looked down at the Star Charm.

It was slowly coming out from beneath the skin around my neck.

I was pushing it out with my fear and hatred and doubt.

I took a deep breath, and then looked into Morabeau's eyes.

"How do you like your chicken done, bro?"

He stared at me confused for a second.

"Me?" I said. "Baby, I like mine *fried*."

I fired two coils of electricity at him. The electricity wrapped around him, lifting his body high off the ground. I released him and he fell in a heap to the ground.

While he was down I tried everything I knew to open the blue bubble that held my aunt prisoner.

"I'm sorry, Charlemagne!" she cried. Tears streamed down her face. "I am so sorry—"

Then I saw her eyes widen in fear.

"Behind you!" she yelled.

I turned.

Morabeau was on his feet, his face dirty, his suit shredded and smoking.

"You've ruined yet another suit, you stupid brat." He looked up at me. Then he sighed and said, "Well, spare the rod, spoil the child. Recess is over, little girl."

From behind his back, he suddenly brought out...

...a black silk top hat and magic wand.

It was the kind of hat and wand that fake magicians use to pull out skinny rabbits, rubber chickens, or fake flowers at kiddie birthday parties. Morabeau tapped the inside of the hat with the wand and made a point of showing me there was nothing inside.

He smiled at me.

Winked.

Did a little tap dance.

Then he tapped the brim of the hat three times—and disappeared.

The hat fell to the ground.

No rabbits hopped out.

No flowers popped up.

Nothing.

I turned back to my aunt.

"Get down!" I shouted. "Move! Get down!"

She crouched as low as she could and I let loose with a spiral of crackling yellow energy at the top of the bubble. The bubble exploded and my aunt fell to the ground, crying and gasping for air.

We hugged.

"I was only doing what I thought was right," she cried. "I never meant for you to get hurt. I didn't mean for any of this to happen—"

Then she screamed.

I turned and looked back at the black silk top hat on the ground.

It was moving.

Shaking.

After a few seconds, a huge lizard's leg with shiny red scales popped out of the hat, its razor-sharp claws tearing at the ground. Then another giant lizard's red-scaled leg popped out of the small hat, its claws digging into the soft ground.

Finally, a red-scaled dragon's head squeezed out, its nostrils flaring and red tentacle mustache wiggling. It looked at me with glowing red eyes and from its ugly fanged mouth it said, "Did you miss me, little one?"

The dragon wiggled the rest of its huge body out of the small hat. From head to tail, it was at least fifty feet long and stood at least ten feet tall.

White smoke curled out of its nostrils and its long, red, forked tongue whipped around, ready to wrap around me and pull me into its big, ugly mouth.

"You sent that Hunter after me and my family," I said. "The Hunter that killed my uncle."

"No," Morabeau the dragon said, stomping toward me, "actually I can't take credit for that. I honestly wish I could, but I can't. The results are the same, however. Bad for Joshua. Good for me. What do they say about timing being everything?" He suddenly let out a terrible roar, and from his nostrils streams of fire shot out at me. "Your time is over!"

I ran.

I ran partly because I wanted to get the dragon as far away from my aunt as possible. But mostly I ran because I didn't know what else to do.

"Ollie, ollie, oxen free!" Morabeau the dragon roared as he ran after me, his dragon feet pounding against the ground.

When I reached the cliff's edge, I jumped and prayed that the rocks and ocean below would be a lot nicer to me than they had been to Trevor.

ENTRY EIGHTEEN:

From Bad to Just-Ain't-Right

Morabeau's red dragon body sailed off the cliff behind me.

Before we hit the water, he began changing from the dragon back to himself. The Breathing Time was almost over. His powers were weakening. As we crashed into the cold, dark ocean water, Morabeau reached out and grabbed my throat. I brought my forearms up between his arms and broke his grip on my neck.

After what seemed like forever under water, Morabeau began desperately swimming for the surface. I followed.

I reached the surface just in time to see Morabeau fly out of the water and grab for the edges of a jagged rock. Waves crashed against the rock, almost washing him back into the water.

For a second, I thought I had landed on the beach.

Until I looked down.

I was *standing* on the water! A wave began rolling in toward the rocks, and I was riding the wave like a surfer without a surf board!

"Yo, hey, Morabeau!" I shouted. "I'm still standing, baby!"

I flew up off of the wave and floated next to Morabeau. He was soaking wet and struggling. There was a deep, bleeding gash in his forehead. He glared at me, coughed, and said, "You vile little creature!"

"Seems like you be needin' some vitamins or something, man," I said. "Maybe more fiber in your diet."

Suddenly he flew off the rock and sailed to the top of the cliff.

I launched myself after him, but not fast enough: by the time I got back to the top of the ridge, Morabeau stood dripping wet over my Aunt Monique with a black crystal bow and arrow in his hands. The bow was drawn back and the arrow was pointing down at my aunt.

"Enough games for one day!" he shouted. "Give me the Star Charm! Now!"

"No, Charlemagne!" Aunt Monique cried out. "Don't do it!"

"Oh, for goodness' sake," Morabeau said to my aunt. "Will you just please shut *up*!"

He fired the arrow into my aunt's chest.

"No!" I screamed.

"That is a black crystal spirit arrow!" Morabeau shouted. "It will drain every bit of life force out of the Princess in less than five minutes! Now you only have two choices, dear girl; we can continue our fight, in which case I'm quite sure five minutes will pass very quickly. Or you can give me the Star Charm now and I will save her life!"

"Okay!" I said, tears blinding my eyes. "Okay! I'm sorry! Please don't let her die!"

I clawed at the Star Charm around my neck. If keeping the Star Charm meant losing my aunt, I didn't want it. It was over. Morabeau won.

I couldn't get the necklace off. There was nothing but the golden tattoo. I clawed at the tattooed skin around my neck. The charm and its necklace were too far beneath my skin. I started to feel it rising through my skin—my fear pushing it out—but it wasn't surfacing fast enough.

I kept clawing at my skin.

"Look at the arrow!" Morabeau shouted. "It's starting to glow white! Two more minutes and the Princess will join your mother and Joshua!"

"I—I can't get it off! Please help her!"

Morabeau rolled his eyes. "Oh, don't tell me it's a latch thing? Why is it women always get necklaces with these itsy-bitsy latches that no one but a Realm Dwelling elf can get? You have one minute!"

"I'm trying! Honest!" I said. "Please don't let her die!"

Nothing I tried worked.

The Star Charm stayed right where it was.

I heard a soft humming sound that grew louder in the sky above.

Morabeau and I both looked up: a shiny black spaceship shaped like an arrowhead was slowly floating down through the early morning sky.

Morabeau suddenly looked frightened.

"See that!" he shouted angrily at me. "That's a Hunter Scout ship! Between me and that Hunter, I'm your only hope of getting out of this alive! Now give me the Star Charm!"

I stopped clawing at my neck.

I stopped crying.

Instead, I gave Morabeau something else: two whirling fireballs. The fireballs exploded at his feet and ripped open the ground. Hot lava bubbled up from the tear in the earth and shot up like an angry fountain.

The lava rained down on Morabeau.

He screamed.

Then...

...his screaming stopped.

The lava fountain boiled and bubbled back into the ground. Morabeau was covered in glowing orange rock. A rock statue staring forever up at the sky in horror.

As the black spaceship slowly hovered closer to the ground, I levitated the rock statue of Morabeau into the air, ready to throw it as far as my powers would let me out into the water, hoping it would sink to the deepest, darkest, most forgotten part of the sea.

"You will never hurt anyone again," I said, feeling myself wanting to cry.

With my last bit of strength I threw the rock statue of Morabeau into the air out over the cliff's edge.

A thin beam of yellow light blazed out from the black spaceship and hit the statue. Morabeau's stone prison exploded into a million bright and burning pieces before raining down into the water below.

A hole opened in the bottom of the ship and a Hunter began floating down to the earth.

"You are the Orisha," the Hunter said, covered from head to foot in his Dark Matter spacesuit. "You will surrender the Star Charm or you will be destroyed."

Someone said, "Not today, Hunter!"

I turned.

Miss Lettie!

Standing with her was Mr. Sheppard.

"Did we miss anything?" Mr. Sheppard asked, ready to fire his Series-7 Energy weapon.

"You possess the Star Charm," the Hunter said. "You will surrender it to me or you will die."

I glanced down at the golden tattoo where the Star Charm had hung around my neck. It was glowing. A soft, golden glow. It flashed blinding white and I was suddenly surrounded by the Goddesses of the Star Charm.

I recognized the goddess Cerridwen.

"Where have you guys been, huh?" I asked angrily. "I coulda used some help earlier, ya know?"

Cerridwen gave a casual shrug.

"You appeared to be doing quite well, your Highness."

"My aunt," I said. "She's hurt. Somebody please—"

"You are the Orisha," the Hunter repeated. "Surrender the Star Charm or die."

The Hunter walked quickly toward me like I was the only red meat on the menu.

Mr. Sheppard fired his energy weapon. The crackling beam was sucked into the Hunter's Dark Matter spacesuit, disappearing without any effect. Miss Lettie let loose with lightning ball after lightning ball at the dark figure coming closer to me. All of the lightning bolts were just sucked into the Hunter's Dark Matter suit.

The Hunter's hand reached out to me. A black lightning bolt rushed out of his hand straight at me.

The goddesses surrounding me joined hands and bowed their heads. The black beam of light hit the circle of women and split into two beams. One of the beams hit the ground and exploded. The other circled around the ring of goddesses and shot straight back at the Hunter. The beam went back inside his hand.

Mr. Sheppard and Miss Lettie continued to fire energy beams and fireballs at the Hunter. Nothing they did worked.

The closer the Hunter got to me, the more I felt an incredible sadness. The sadness grew until I finally shouted to Miss Lettie and Mr. Sheppard, "Stop!"

"It's a Hunter, your Highness!" Mr. Sheppard shouted, firing another blast of bright yellow energy.

"Stop!" I shouted again. "I command you! Please…"

This time they did.

I walked through the circle of goddesses toward the Hunter.

"Charlemagne," a voice in the shadows said. "Please go no further."

My heart skipped a beat.

From the shadows a man appeared. He was wearing a black cloak and carried an energy staff like the one Mr. Sheppard had been firing.

"Uncle Joshua?" I heard myself say.

"Please, Charlemagne," Uncle Joshua said, walking closer to the Hunter. "Move away from the Hunter now."

"But, Uncle—"

"Now, your Highness!"

I felt my body jerk and I took a frightened step back.

The Hunter turned away from me to and slowly stretched his arm out toward Uncle Joshua. Uncle Joshua fired his energy staff. The blast knocked the Hunter off his feet. The chest of the Dark Matter suit splashed open for a second before closing.

"Stop it!" I shouted. "You're killing him!"

"That's the point, your Highness!" Uncle Joshua said, firing another blast at the fallen Hunter. The chest of the Dark Matter suit splashed open again before quickly sealing itself.

I stepped between Uncle Joshua and the Hunter lying on the ground.

"I beg of you to move, your Highness," Uncle Joshua said.

"No," I said.

Uncle Joshua looked at me, his eyes pleading.

"Charlemagne," he said quietly. "I have sworn my life to protect you. Please let me—"

"No," I said, looking back at the fallen Hunter. "He's been hurt enough."

I turned to Miss Lettie and said, "Please help my aunt. She's hurt real bad."

"I will spare no powers, your Highness," Miss Lettie said before she ran off to where my aunt lay.

The Hunter sat up. He struggled to his feet and I looked up into his dark helmet only to see my reflection.

"Charlemagne," Uncle Joshua said sternly.

"It's okay," I said.

Slowly, I raised my hand and started to touch the Dark Matter helmet.

"Your Highness!" Mr. Sheppard shouted. "No!"

Too late.

I touched the helmet.

"You... are... the ... Orisha," the Hunter said.

The helmet was cold. Colder than anything I'd ever felt before. Through the cold I felt sadness and fear.

"It's okay," I said. "I can help."

"Surrender... the Star... Charm..."

With my hand still touching the Hunter's helmet the Dark Matter began melting away, dripping like thick black oil to the ground, forming a pool at his feet.

What had been inside the Dark Matter spacesuit collapsed unconscious to the ground.

A boy.

He couldn't have been much older than me. Maybe thirteen or fourteen.

He looked a little alien but mostly human, especially the eyes and the mouth. I had no idea where his nose was, but there was no doubt he was just a boy.

When he came to, he was crying. He opened his eyes, saw me, and in fear tried to crawl away. Uncle Joshua pressed the tip of his energy staff at the boy's temple. Gently, I pushed the weapon away.

"It's okay," I said, kneeling beside the boy. "I'm a friend. Can you understand me?"

He quickly nodded and pointed to the back of his head. "I have the lobe," he said.

"The what?"

"Language translator lobe," Mr. Sheppard said. "A small, artificially grown organism placed at the base of the brain. Helps the brain instantly understand a number of alien languages. Kind of looks like an oyster. We all have one. Including you, your Highness."

Gee.

Even *more* stuff that promised to keep me wide awake at night.

"Who are you?" I asked the boy. "Why are you trying to hurt me?"

The boy looked nervously around at Uncle Joshua, Mr. Sheppard, and me. Before long he started talking.

The Hunters—nearly all of them—were just kids. The children of slaves. Sky Conjurers who had been captured and made to work in mines and forests and farming fields spread out across the galaxy. These were the Sky Conjurers who had not been lucky enough to escape.

The children were taken from their families and made to wear Dark Matter suits; suits that held them prisoner inside their greatest fear: the fear that they would never see their parents again. The fear that they would be left all alone in this great, big, cold universe unless they searched the far, dark corners of space for the Star Charm.

"You have to let me take it!" the boy cried. "If you don't, they'll kill my parents! Please! Let me have it! You don't need it!"

Mr. Sheppard reached a paw down over the boy's head. His paw began glowing purple. The boy stopped crying and soon fell asleep.

"What do we do with this stuff?" Mr. Sheppard asked, looking down at the twisting, wiggling pool of Dark Matter. "Nothing I know can hold it. Then again," Mr. Sheppard said, eyeing Uncle Joshua with suspicion, "I never heard of a weapon that could do what yours did, Joshua."

"You would not have heard of it, Altarian, since you are not of the Ashanti Kai Body," Uncle Joshua said, still holding his weapon near the boy. "An Ashanti Kai *Toth Viper* wand. Only the best Ashanti Kai are given such weapons."

"We will hold the Dark Matter."

It was a goddess named Yemaya.

Yemaya stepped out from the circle and held out a golden glass jar. The black, oily pool rose up like a black snake and slid into the golden jar. Yemaya put a top on the jar, smiled, and bowed to me.

I hugged Uncle Joshua.

"I missed you so much," I said, hugging him tighter and tighter just to make sure he was real.

I stepped away and looked up at him.

Mr. Sheppard was holding his energy weapon on Uncle Joshua.

"It was you, wasn't it, Joshua," Mr. Sheppard said.

"What are you talking about?" I asked turning to Mr. Sheppard.

"It's all right, your Highness," Uncle Joshua said. "You're right, Altarian. It was me. Perhaps you might have made a fine Ashanti Kai Knight after all."

"What's going on?" I asked.

"He's the one who hacked into the Sentinel outposts," Mr. Sheppard said, still holding his weapon on my uncle. "He's the one who sent the message out to attract a Hunter Scout. For as weak as the signal was, it was also very exact. Whatever Hunter picked it up would've had no choice but to follow it here to the pinpoint location of your old apartment building in the City. Is that about right, Joshua?"

Uncle Joshua bowed to Mr. Sheppard and said, "I can see why Queen Yolanda trusted you entirely. You are very perceptive."

"Why?" I asked Uncle Joshua.

"Whatever her faults, Princess Monique was right about one thing: None of us should have to live the way we do on Earth or anywhere else," Uncle Joshua said. "I served your mother as a handpicked Ashanti Kai Knight. A secret warrior. One who could be trusted to work alone for the greater good. You, your Highness, are the greater good. I was to protect you and your aunt. But you, first and foremost."

"You're—not my uncle?" I said.

The man I'd known as Uncle Joshua bowed his head and said, "No, your Highness."

"You sent the message to Miss Lettie to come help at the apartment that night, didn't you?" Mr. Sheppard said. "You're a telepath. How else could she have known you were under a Hunter attack? But she can usually sense who sends her telepathic messages—"

"It has long been my job to live undetected," Uncle Joshua said.

"You sent for Miss Lettie because you knew you could trust her to protect the queen," Mr. Sheppard said. "And you pretended to die that night so that you could be free to work as the Ashanti Kai truly do. Undetected. Invisible. Without a name or home or family."

"You saved us from the third Bokuban back in the bayou," I said. "Didn't you?"

Again, the man I had known as Uncle Joshua bowed and said, "Yes, your Highness. I have never been very far from your side." Slowly, he raised his head and looked at me. "Forgive me the pain I've caused you, your Highness. All of this is my doing. But you had to be tested. And through this test, the Sky Conjuring People in exile on this world have been shown the fulfillment of the prophecies. You are the one we have waited a thousand years for. You are the Orisha."

I stared at him for a long time.

"I hate you," I said. I ran to Miss Lettie and my aunt.

How could Uncle Joshua—or whoever he was—have put me through such an awful test? How could he have lied to us?

To me!

My aunt lay on the ground, her head in Miss Lettie's lap. Miss Lettie was holding the now glowing white crystal arrow in her hand. I knelt by my aunt's side. Miss Lettie looked at me and shook her head.

My aunt's eyes fluttered open for a moment.

She tried to smile.

"My baby," she said. "Please forgive…"

Then, she was gone.

ENTRY NINETEEN:

On This You Must Believe...

"Is this how you wish her to be?"

Miss Lettie and I looked up.

Standing over us was a woman wearing a gown made from bright, colorful bird feathers.

"Who are you?" I said.

"I am the goddess Pachamama," she said. "Is this how you wish her to be?"

"No," I said, feeling hot tears burning my cheeks. "Of course not."

"I offer healing," Pachamama said. "Your aunt's conjuring power is forever gone, but her life force has not crossed over yet. If it is healing you wish for her, then you must command me."

"But Miss Lettie tried everything—"

"Miss Lettie," Pachamama said, "is a gifted child in the world of enchantment. But what is beyond her growing powers is easily within my reach." Again, she looked at my aunt, then at me, and said, "Is this how you wish her to be?"

"No."

"Then I await your command," Pachamama said.

"Please," is all I could say.

Pachamama nodded once. A large white feather appeared in her hand. She knelt, said a few strange words, and passed the feather gently over my aunt from her head to her feet. Aunt Monique suddenly gasped. She was breathing again.

"Now, she must rest," Pachamama said. Then she nodded once to Miss Lettie and floated back to the circle of goddesses.

The goddesses all separated into individual beams of golden light and drifted back into the Star Charm sunk beneath the skin of my neck.

"Excuse me," Mr. Sheppard called out to us. He was pointing up to the Dark Matter spaceship floating in the air above him. "What the heck are we supposed to do with *this* thing?"

ENTRY TWENTY:

Healing

We carried Aunt Monique to friends of Miss Lettie: a woman named Miss N'Dego and a woman named Miss Chooch. Miss Lettie said they were both something called *izan'goma*—traditional Sky Conjurer healers that used only natural plants, herbs, and old-school magic spells to heal the sick.

Miss N'Dego had to be older than dirt—even older than Miss Evelyn. She was short and round, with skin like dark, shiny molasses. She wore a bright flowered island dress and matching bandana. I don't think she had any teeth.

Miss Chooch was much younger and looked like she was Mexican with beautiful reddish gold skin and waist-long hair as black and as shiny as Dark Matter.

"We help da Princess recover," Miss N'Dego said, smiling a toothless smile. "Feeds her vegetables from Miss Lettie's garden, gives her my own special herbal tea."

I nodded to Miss Chooch and asked, "What's your partner do?"

"Miss Chooch?" Miss N'Dego said. "Oh, she stand outside da Princess's dream gate. Heal da dreams comin' in and goin' out."

"She can do that?" I asked.

"Makes good soup, too," Miss N'Dego said, winking at me.

I told Uncle Joshua to stay with Aunt Monique. He wasn't happy about his assignment. He said I was the one that had to be protected. I told him Mr. Sheppard was guarding me and that he should do what I asked. I think I was trying to punish Uncle Joshua for having made me believe with my whole heart in all of his lies—even if all of his lies had been for my own good.

The boy who had been trapped inside the Dark Matter suit stayed at Miss Lettie's house.

He slept for three full days.

For one of those days, he tossed and turned, moaned and sweated like he was full of fever and nightmares. Miss Lettie sat with him, wiping the sweat from his forehead, cooling him with a cold cloth. On the second day, Miss Chooch the Mexican-looking lady stopped by and stood over his bed for a couple of hours. By the time she left, he was in a deep sleep.

"Very bad dreams," she said. "They're gone now. He will sleep well." Miss Chooch saw me staring at her. She smiled at me and said, "You should try my cheese-tortilla soup, too, your Highness."

When the boy woke up, he was hungry. We fed him and kept feeding him until he couldn't eat any more.

His name was Masi and he came from a planet called Oban Sha'Cree. The Purifiers had invaded his world, made the people slaves, and used them to mine a special metal that made Oban Sha'Cree an enchanted planet.

"If I stay, the Purifiers will send another scout ship into this region—perhaps more than a scout ship," Masi said. "They will come this time for you, Queen Charlemagne. And nothing—not Sky Conjurers or the humans—will stand in their way."

Miss Lettie, Mr. Sheppard, and I talked in private about what to do. I didn't want to send him back. He was just a boy and he deserved to live freely and without fear.

Mr. Sheppard saw no other choice but to send him back into deep space. Back into the hive of Hunters searching other planets for the Star Charm and me. Masi would be missed by the Hunters, argued Mr. Sheppard. And when one Hunter was missing, an army would come looking for him.

"I have decided for you," Masi said, standing in the doorway. He had heard every word we had said. "I must go back. There are too many others like me. Other children held prisoner inside the Dark Matter suits. I cannot abandon them. I will wear the suit and fight against its powers."

"Maybe we can kick that strength up a notch," I said.

I stood back, closed my eyes and slowed my breathing.

"Yes, your Highness?"

I opened my eyes.

It was Cerridwen.

"Do you or any of my other home-girl goddesses know how we can help protect Masi after he puts the Dark Matter suit back on?" I asked.

Cerridwen bowed to me and said, "As you command."

Cerridwen disappeared and in her place stood a very pretty, muscular woman with long black hair and copper-colored skin. She wore a short white chiffon dress and carried a golden bow and arrows.

"I am Artemis," the woman said, bowing to me. "You wish my help?"

"Not me," I said. I pointed to Masi. "Him."

"So be it," Artemis said.

Quickly, she slipped an arrow in her bow and drew it back.

"Whoa, whoa, whoa!" I said holding my hands up and stepping in front of the arrow. "Okay, see, like, since my aunt got stuck with one of those things, I'm not a big fan of arrows, n'k?"

"I give strength to believe in one's self," she said. "To be strong in spirit against all that would weaken it. I help to give courage where there was none and hope where darkness has fallen. My arrows deliver such strength to the noble directly to their hearts."

I looked at Masi.

Masi bowed and said, "I am ready."

"Okay," I said stepping aside. "Do your business, girl."

Artemis drew back her bow and released the arrow. The arrow hit the middle of Masi's chest and instantly dissolved into him. He took in a sharp, deep breath, then looked down to where a hole should have been but wasn't. He looked up at us as if he was seeing us for the first time.

Artemis bowed to me, said, "Your Highness," then disappeared.

"How do you feel?" Miss Lettie asked Masi.

He nodded to her and said, "Strong."

Later that evening, Cerridwen gave the golden glass jar with the Dark Matter in it to Masi. Miss Lettie, Mr. Sheppard, and I were standing outside the main door of his Dark Matter spaceship.

"You sure you want to do this?" Miss Lettie asked Masi.

"My mother, father, and sister are out there, slaves to the Purifiers," Masi said. "Yes, your Highness, I am sure I want to do this."

Masi took in a deep breath and poured the Dark Matter over his head. The black sludge dripped down over him and took the shape of a black helmet and spacesuit.

"You okay in there?" I asked, tapping on the helmet's black visor.

"I am strong," he said. "Please stop tapping."

He turned and began walking up the ramp to his ship.

"Hunter! Stop!" It was Uncle Joshua. "I'm going with you."

"What?" I felt my heart drop into my stomach. "But you— you can't."

"I must," Uncle Joshua said. "There is little else I can do here, your Highness. Your powers far exceed what protection I can give. And the Princess is in safe hands. I can be of more use to you out there."

"I've always liked you, Joshua," Mr. Sheppard said. "I don't trust you as far as I can throw the Crystal Towers of Forgonath left-pawed with the wind in my face and sun in my eyes. But I like you. Just thought you should know."

Uncle Joshua smiled at Mr. Sheppard and said, "And that is why you would have made a good Ashanti Kai warrior." Still speaking to Mr. Sheppard, Uncle Joshua pointed to me and said, "Look after the queen. She is our future."

I ran up to Uncle Joshua and hugged him.

I was glad to feel his arms around me, hugging me back.

He knelt on one knee and looked at me.

"It has been a pleasure, your Highness," he said.

"I love you," I said.

"Be good, Charlemagne," he said. He kissed my cheek and said, "That is from me." Then he kissed my hand and said, "And this is from your loyal servant."

He stood and walked up the ship's ramp with Masi. My feet started moving. Slowly at first, then into a run. I stopped at the bottom of the ship's black ramp.

"Hey!" I said. He stopped and turned to me. "Did you—do you know who my father is?"

He didn't answer for a long time.

"Yes," he said.

The question in my chest kept swelling, growing larger and aching.

"Is he—alive?" I said.

"Very much so."

"Is he—" I swallowed hard, "—you?"

The man I had known as Uncle Joshua looked at me for a very long time. Then he said, "Search your heart."

I did.

And there it was. The truth. A truth that instantly filled me with happiness and sadness.

"Guard the queen," he finally said to Miss Lettie and Mr. Sheppard. "Protect her. Guide her. She is what we have all hoped for." He smiled at me and said, "She is all *I* have ever hoped for."

"What's your real name?" I said.

He looked confused for a minute before he said, "It's been so long, I can't—" Then he paused, looked at me, and said, "Give me my name, your Highness."

I took his hands in mine and said, "Joshua. Joshua Mack."

"A good name," he said, before kissing me on my cheek. "A warrior's name."

Then he turned and walked into the darkness of the Dark Matter ship.

Miss Lettie, Mr. Sheppard, and I watched the black Hunter scout ship glide high into the air. In the blink of an eye, it became a small and quickly fading star.

Miss Lettie put her arm around my shoulder.

"Did you know?" I asked, looking up at her. "I mean about him being my father?"

"Dey be secret places in de heart even de most powerful magic cannot reveal," she said. "No, your Highness. I did not know."

The three of us—Miss Lettie, Mr. Sheppard, and I—watched the sky in silence for a very long time.

"We will see dem again," Miss Lettie finally said.

I nodded and said, "I know."

ENTRY TWENTY-ONE:

The Beginning

"What you have set in motion," Lona said, "cannot be undone. If this is truly the path your Highness wishes to follow, then we as the Sky Conjuring Council shall walk with you."

"It would be an honor to have the Council at my side," I said, standing in front of the Council members. "I know I'm kinda new at this queen thing. But I was an Honors student at my old school—I mean, until I got kicked out. I guess what I'm trying to say is I'm a fast learner and I'm not afraid of homework. I want to do my part to help. That's not just a Sky Conjurer thing. It's a human thing, too."

Lona smiled at me and said, "You have proven yourself beyond what we asked for in our prayers. A good reason to give thanks at the ceremony."

"What ceremony?" I asked. I turned and looked at Miss Lettie and Mr. Sheppard. They were smiling.

"It is the ceremony," Lona said, "where we officially pronounce you, Charlemagne Althea Mack, as our Queen. Your coronation."

"Is there, like, an after-party?" I said.

"The biggest party you have ever seen," Lona said. She tapped the huge wind chime and the meeting ended.

Miss Lettie, Mr. Sheppard, and I walked down the long hallway toward the cave's exit. I said, "How come you guys didn't give me the 4-1-1 on this ceremony thing?"

"We figured dey be time enough to inform you after the Council meeting," Miss Lettie said.

"Besides, the ceremony is all the way on the other side of the island," Mr. Sheppard said. "A ten-mile hike through Lakshmi Valley, two miles through the Elysian rain forest, then—"

"Awright," I said. "I get the idea. Did I happen to mention that I'm not exactly into hiking?"

"I thought you might say something like that, your Highness," Mr. Sheppard said as we came out of the cave and into daylight. Parked outside of the cave was a very big, very shiny, and very cool white spaceship.

"The queen's personal Starchaser," Mr. Sheppard said. "It was your mother's. Now, your Highness, it's yours."

Tears flooded my eyes.

I couldn't believe it.

"I, uh—I kept many of her things inside," Mr. Sheppard said. "In case you—you know—"

I hugged him so hard I think I heard him gagging. Then I kissed his wet black nose.

I stood and hugged Miss Lettie.

"Well?" Miss Lettie said. "Don't we have a party to get to?"

I ran up the long, white ramp and into the ship.

Just inside the doorway there was a three-dimensional photo of my mother's face.

It was the first photo I'd ever seen of her.

She was beautiful.

I touched the photo.

"Hello, baby-girl," the photo said.

I jumped back.

"Your touch is all that was needed to activate this image," she said. "Your being here means your journey as queen has just begun. Know that I will always be with you. You must not look back at what could have been. You must now look forward to what must be accomplished. Stay strong, my sweet baby-girl. Become the queen you were destined to be."

The image went quiet and became just a 3-D photo of my beautiful, beautiful mother again.

I looked at Miss Lettie.

She put her hand on my shoulder, then smiled and nodded. M r. Sheppard sat at the controls of the Starchaser. It was easy to see he was very happy running his paws over the lights, levers, buttons, and switches of the control panel.

Behind him, in the middle of the control room, was a big, white chair up on a round platform. The chair looked like a huge white tulip in bloom. I looked at Miss Lettie and she nodded. I sat in the chair. The chair where my mother used to sit.

Miss Lettie took a seat next to Mr. Sheppard at the main control panel. He fired up the engines.

"Can I drive?" I said.

"No," they said.

We lifted quickly into the air, and through the windows I saw the island dropping beneath us.

"Feels good to be back in the saddle, eh, Miss Lettie?" Mr. Sheppard said.

"Feels good, Mr. Sheppard," Miss Lettie said.

"Let's ride, y'all," I said.

Mr. Sheppard punched the engines.

And, girl, we were out…

The day after the ceremony, Lona showed me to my new home: the Queen's Royal Residence. A huge white and yellow house set on top of a hill at the foot of Tutu Biko Mountain. The rooms were filled with cushy sofas and silk pillows and white lace curtains catching breezes off the sea. There were small fountains, candles, wind chimes, tall flowers in big vases, and a library full of old books, star maps, paintings, and sculptures.

It was everything I always thought I wanted.

After one night at the house, it turned out to be nothing I wanted at all.

It felt lonely. Too far away from everybody.

My aunt was still in the care of Miss N'Dego and Miss Chooch at Miss Chooch's small house near the marketplace. Aunt Monique was dealing with a lot of guilty feelings, horrible dreams, and the loss of her conjuring powers. It would be a while before she truly believed I'd forgiven her and that I loved her no matter what. I asked Lona if it would be all right if my aunt, Miss N'Dego, and Miss Chooch moved into the queen's house.

"And where will you live, your Highness?" Lona asked.

Miss Lettie wasn't sure what to think when I asked if I could live with her. After all, how would you feel if a queen asked if she could crash in your spare bedroom?

At first she was real nervous. It didn't take her long, though, to start smacking my elbows off the kitchen table when I ate and telling me things like, "Sit up straight, child," and "Chimpanzees walk like dat—you ain't no chimpanzee," and "A queen does not 'fart'—she sprinkles daisies."

Since things have been pretty quiet the past week, I've had time to think. Really think. Mostly I wonder about what kind of person—what kind of queen—I'll be a year from now. Five years from now. I wonder what it'll feel like to read this journal when I'm, like, thirteen, or even eighteen.

So much has happened.

So much is *going* to happen.

Everybody seems to think of me as some sort of hero. I'm not. The real heroes are the people who believed in me no matter what. Miss Lettie. Mr. Sheppard. Miss Evelyn. Mr. Trinidad. Miss Peekaboo. My dad, Joshua Mack. My mom, Queen Yolanda. Even my aunt.

Right now, I'm sitting on the beach in front of Miss Lettie's house. Our house. She's just waved for me to come up. We're going to the marketplace for a few things, including more blank journal books since I'm almost out of room in this one.

After shopping, Moya Akora—my best little five-year-old girlfriend—and I are gonna see how much ice cream we can each eat without getting brain-freezes. Then the rest of the day's going to be spent at the St. Hestia Public Library studying Enchantment Arts History, Sky Conjurer Social Studies, and the first of 923 books that make up *The Book of Legends*.

Just when you think school's out…

…it's only just started.

THE END